The All-the-Way Man

by

JOYCE DINGWELL

Harlequin Books

TORONTO • LONDON • LOS ANGELES • AMSTERDAM
SYDNEY • HAMBURG • PARIS • STOCKHOLM • ATHENS • TOKYO

Original hardcover edition published in 1980
by Mills & Boon Limited

ISBN 0-373-02432-0

Harlequin edition published October 1981

Copyright © 1980 by Joyce Dingwell.
Philippine copyright 1980. Australian copyright 1980.
All rights reserved. Except for use in any review, the reproduction or utilization
of this work in whole or in part in any form by any electronic, mechanical or
other means, now known or hereafter invented, including xerography,
photocopying and recording, or in any information storage or retrieval system,
is forbidden without the permission of the publisher, Harlequin Enterprises
Limited, 225 Duncan Mill Road, Don Mills, Ontario, Canada M3B 3K9. All the
characters in this book have no existence outside the imagination of the
author and have no relation whatsoever to anyone bearing the same name
or names. They are not even distantly inspired by any individual known
or unknown to the author, and all the incidents are pure invention.

The Harlequin trademark, consisting of the words HARLEQUIN ROMANCE
and the portrayal of a Harlequin, is registered in the United States Patent
Office and in the Canada Trade Marks Office.

Printed in U.S.A.

"I want her to see us together."

Tim stepped closer as he spoke. "Godmother will get the message about us when she sees us slinking into the dark. Come on, woman, slink!"

To her dismay, Jessica was urged into the shadows. The light that was on in godmother's room suddenly went out.

"Now that you've succeeded, may I return to the house?" Jessica asked contemptuously.

"No," Tim refused. "I want godmother to sweat it out a little longer. Meanwhile, I have a complaint to make. You didn't play your role very well tonight."

"How could I?" objected Jessica. "You were so corny about everything— kissing me at the window, for instance, when a genuine lover would have sought out the dark."

"Like this dark?" he interpreted as he bent to kiss her. And he held the kiss. . . .

JOYCE DINGWELL
is also the author of these
Harlequin Romances

Many of these titles are available at your local bookseller.

For a free catalogue listing all available Harlequin Romances
and Harlequin Presents, send your name and address to:

HARLEQUIN READER SERVICE
1440 South Priest Drive, Tempe, AZ 85281
Canadian address: Stratford, Ontario N5A 6W2

CHAPTER ONE

IT was mid-afternoon by the time the small air-craft approached the blur of buildings in the middle of the sweep of plains, and Jessica, peering over a wing, sighed deeply: 'Journey's end!'

She certainly hoped it was, for she had been flying since daybreak, and she was tired.

She was fairly confident, however, for her brother's letters had been fully confident; without Toby's: 'This place is a home away from home . . . I know you would love it . . . I feel sure Tim would welcome you and find you a job . . .' she would not have come. Not all the way from Sydney to Central Australia, and then to Saffron Downs.

Jessica had been unemployed for months, fast advancing from the apprehensive stage to the near-desperate, and her twin's encouraging words had sent her rummaging for her bags. Without waiting for any particulars, without ascertaining what kind of job, not asking anything at all, not even warning Toby, she had packed and left.

It had seemed right at the time, it had seemed right·for the entire journey, but——

But now, looking nervously ahead to S.D. . . . 'Everyone,' Toby had also written, 'speaks of Saffron Downs as S.D.' . . . Jessica suddenly was not so sure.

What was it really like, this S.D.? she wondered. Was it as pleasant as Toby had described? Would she be welcome? Could it prove to be a home away from home?

No, no and no. This time Jessica was quite sure of her answers. No place of that *over*-size, she decided, could ever be anything of the sort.

She shivered and closed her eyes.

'What is it?' The friendly young pilot at the controls was evidently looking at her. He had picked her up at Alice Springs after she had approached him and told him she was expected at Saffron Downs. He said he had not been briefed, but since she said so, hop in.

Jessica had hopped.

It had been a wonderful journey for her. Actually for the first time she had been conscious of space. After the confinement of a crowded city, a cramped fourth share in a smallish flat, more recently this morning's lesser wheatlands, reduced sheeplands, the incredible vastness of the cattle country had grabbed at her. She had been aware of a new freedom, new air to breathe, new room to stretch and expand. She had felt quite wonderful, until——

'You don't look as cocky as you did before.' The young pilot . . . Jeff . . . was evidently regarding her again. 'Anything wrong?'

'Yes,' Jessica gulped, her eyes still closed. 'It's big.' She nodded blindly ahead.

'Of course it's big,' he came back. 'It has to be for sixty thousand head of branded cattle and one thousand horses.'

'How—how many thousands of people?' Jessica faltered, but the pilot's answer cheered her.

'People? Are you joking? There's only a handful of them.'

At once Jessica was relieved. She had not wanted a large place. When Toby had left Sydney for the Centre she had been obliged to forfeit their cosy cottage and share community digs, something that was far from intimate and a home away from home. Now she was yearning for simple living again.

But it seemed, if this Jeff was right, that she was to have her wish after all, in spite of that depressing over-size. With a smile Jessica opened her eyes ... then promptly shut them again. Over-size? The place was positively monstrous!

She started to say so, but the pilot called out that he was going down. Deciding to look out, Jessica saw that they were losing height.

She peered eagerly earthwards, searching for the upturned white plastic buckets that her brother had written always marked these outback run-ins. She found none. But she did note a formal, sealed strip. The hangar at the far end of the field, too, was a formal building, nothing like the old brown barn that Toby had described in his letters. Also, coming closer to the ground, that smart four-wheel-drive definitely was not the dusty jalopy that Toby had described.

About to ask if this indeed was S.D., Jessica saw the letters on the rippling wind sock, and they were clearly that. There was S.D., too, marked in giant letters on the tarmac. Yes, it had to be Saffron Downs.

'Is it what you expected?' Jeff had the engine cut by now, and was looking at Jessica's dubious face with intrigue.

'Yes. No,' Jessica said hollowly.

'What does that mean?' he asked.

'The country is like I thought it would be, but S.D. is not. I mean' . . . more hollowly . . . 'its size.'

'Oh, the size again, is it? You expected a country dump, did you?'

'Something like that. I certainly didn't anticipate a city!'

Jeff gave a sympathetic nod. 'I suppose it does come as a shock at first to a newchum, but you'll get used to it. After all, it has to be big, it's the hub for a hell of a big concern. You're in luck, I see, the big boss himself has come out to collect you, and not your brother.' Jessica, during the flight, had spoken of Toby. 'What did you say your brother's name was?'

'I didn't, but it's Makin. Toby Makin.'

'I can't recall any Makin, but then he wouldn't be in my line, would he?'

'No, Toby is the paymaster.'

'Is he then?' Jeff looked at her quizzically. 'Well, I should know Makin the paymaster, shouldn't I? But I don't. But not to worry, I'll certainly be recalling the name of Makin from now on.' He gave Jessica a long appreciative look. He hopped down from the Cessna and came round to help her off. As he did so he said: 'You still look doubtful. Isn't the boss expecting you?'

'Not exactly, but Toby said that he—well, he

told me——'

'Yes,' agreed Jeff, 'Tim is a decent sort.'

Tim. Immediately Jessica felt confident again. Toby had said Tim, so everything was all right. For a moment she had thought ... had wondered ...

She waited while Jeff removed her bags, and as she did so she became progressively and sharply aware that she was being watched, watched very closely. She did not turn to check if her feeling was only imagination; nor did she turn to see who, if someone did look, was looking. There was only one person who could look, and he was the man who had come out in the waggon. The big boss, Jeff had said.

But he was also Tim, Jessica prompted herself, Tim who according to Toby, would welcome her and find her a job; Tim who, according to the pilot, was a decent sort.

A boss and a decent sort certainly called for acknowledgment. Accordingly Jessica made herself turn round.

'Good afternoon,' she called.

At least the man did not reject her. He said: 'Miss,' and gave the briefest movement of a dark head beneath a large felt hat. His intensely blue eyes under the hat, blue even from the distance between them, never left Jessica's face. They were slitted, but Jessica sensed that that was not because of the brilliant western sunlight but because he was waiting for her to explain her presence.

'I'm Jessica Makin,' she told him.

'So?' he said.

'Makin. M-a-k-i-n.' In spite of herself Jessica said it a little resentfully; she had certainly expected more of a response than 'So?' After all, Makin was not Jones or Smith, and even in a place much bigger than Toby had given her to expect, surely an employer must know the name of his paymaster?

'I'm the sister of Toby Makin,' she went on, waiting for a flicker of recognition, for Toby was an outgoing, knowable person, everyone took to her twin. Yet here was someone who obviously did not know Toby, so had not taken to him. It was a distinct letdown, and Jessica visibly slumped.

If he noticed her deflation, the man made no sign.

'Go on,' he invited coolly.

'Toby told me to come,' Jessica blurted. 'He said Tim would welcome me and find me a job.'

'I'm Tim.'

'Oh!' Jessica could think of nothing else to say.

But the man had not run out of words. He continued at once: 'There is no job.' His voice was stony.

Jerked out of any diplomacy, Jessica heard herself retorting angrily: 'And no welcome, either!'

'Did you expect one?' he asked. 'I don't know you, and I certainly never invited you, and before you remind me of western hospitality, remember there's a time and a place.'

Jessica said bitterly: 'I believed this was the place.'

'Why should you believe that?' the man demanded.

'My brother said so,' Jessica replied.

'The one named Makin, M-a-k-i-n?' he sneered.

'Yes.' Jessica stood bewildered, not knowing what to say or do.

The man, very tall, very large, very brown, very *everything*, watched her curiously.

'What else did this very imaginative person say?' he inquired.

'Toby is not imaginative, he's a realist. And yet——' Jessica's puzzled voice stammered into silence.

'Yes?'

'And yet he told me that S.D. was home from home.' She looked around.

'Now that's very folksy of him,' the man applauded falsely.

'That's what I thought,' Jessica agreed. 'That's why I flew out.'

'From where, miss?'

'Sydney.'

'Not waiting to tell this imaginary person you were coming, I take it?' The eyes were widening slightly now, and the bright blue was quite startling.

'Toby is actual,' Jessica defended.

'Not warning him of your visit?' the man persisted, ignoring the defence.

'No.'

'Not asking permission?'

'N-no.'

'Just expecting to be accepted?'

'Well—yes,' Jessica agreed.

'Then you can damn well get back with Jeff and go home again,' came the immediate response.

'Home?' Jessica said faintly.

'Alice Springs, then ... wherever you came from.'

'Sydney—I told you.'

'Then Sydney. Also jump to it, please. Jeff has to get to The Alice before dark. Throw in your bags and hop on.'

'But I can't!' Jessica protested urgently. 'I have no place to go to ... I forfeited my share in a flat when I came here.'

'Then you'll have to find more digs, won't you?'

'I can't,' Jessica said again. 'I mean, I couldn't without a job. You see, I haven't any money. I spent all I had on this trip. Mr—Mr Tim, isn't it?' She looked at him plaintively.

'Tim,' he nodded, unmoved.

'Mr Tim, I can't go back.'

'No? Well, I'm not having you. You see, Miss Makin ... it is Makin, isn't it? ... neither I nor Saffron Downs want you. It's as simple and basic as that.'

'But——'

'Listen, Jessie Makin.' Jessica winced at the 'Jessie', but he ignored her aversion. 'Listen ... then get the hell out.' He thumped the palm of his right hand with his left fist with considerable force.

'I am listening,' Jessica gulped.

'Saffron Downs' . . . he looked indicatively around, and Jessica perforce looked with him . . . 'is a place that doesn't go in for women. Not because it's too hot and too tough for them, from my experience women are not the delicate flowers they like to be thought, but because I want it that way.'

'But Toby said——'

'I don't care what your brother said, nor do I know how he could say it when he isn't here.' A sudden, abrupt silence, a very long, very contemplative silence. 'That is, unless . . . yes, unless . . .'

'Please?' Jessica looked eagerly at the man.

'Unless,' came the reply, 'he works at a *different* station.'

'Oh, no, it's S.D., Saffron Downs, I'm quite sure of that.'

'By a different station I meant a different S.D. station, not some other concern. You see, I have two more.'

'Two more!' she exclaimed.

'Three altogether. This one, as you must see, is the big apple.'

'Yes, I see that,' Jessica agreed. She, too, was looking thoughtful. 'Meaning,' she deduced presently, 'that Toby's S.D. *could* be the home from home that he said, not like this at all.'

'It could be,' he shrugged, 'but I'm not taking his word, or your report, on that, not till I check with my paymaster.'

'Toby is the paymaster.'

'Thank you for telling me,' he drawled. 'It's interesting to learn about one's staff—from an outsider.'

'It's the truth, Mr—Tim. Toby *is* the paymaster. I've had a letter from him every week.'

'Yet you showed neither the sense nor the good manners to write back and tell him you were coming.'

'That,' Jessica admitted, 'was a mistake.'

'A damn big mistake, and one I'm not allowing to go any further. Get into the waggon and we'll kill this thing at once.'

'But——' she began.

'*Get in!*' he fairly yelled. Her startled jump back from him evidently made him pull himself together.

'Look,' he said in a faintly milder voice, 'if you'd done things the civilised way, written to me, asked me could you join your brother——'

'You still would have said no,' Jessica reminded him, 'because you don't take women.'

'Not here, no, but I might have considered it out there. But you didn't, did you, you went your own merry way.'

'Merry!' Now it was Jessica who shouted. 'You call my life in Sydney merry? It's easy for your sort, the beef sort, to say that, you're hundreds of miles away—*and rich*. But down there a lot of us exist from day to day. There's what they call a depression. Ever heard of that, Mr Moneybags Cattleman? No? Then it's time you did. It's time you gave it some thought.'

'And you give this some thought,' he thundered back. 'The beef just now is down so low the cattlemen are closing up right and left. Those who haven't shut their gates are just sitting around praying for a break.'

'It looks like it,' Jessica managed to insert, gazing significantly at the scene around her.

'I'm one of the lucky ones,' he bellowed, 'perhaps the only lucky one left around here after four disastrous seasons. Most of the other fellows have left, and that isn't funny, it's sad. We have an old Western saying. It's: "Beef breeds tough boys." Believe me, beef *does* do that, Jessie Makin, and things have to reach rock bottom for a cattleman to shut his gates.' He closed his mouth with a snap and waited for her onslaught.

But Jessica would have been tough herself if she had not caught the faintly cracked note in his voice as he spoke of 'the other fellows.' At once, even though she hated him for his treatment of her, her defences were down.

She found she could not entirely withdraw, however, so contented herself with murmuring: 'I've changed my mind. I'll leave, of course.'

'On what?' Again he was yelling, but yelling too late; Jeff, deciding that he was needed no longer, was already taxiing down the strip. Before they could raise a united shout to stop him, before they could wave their arms, the Cessna found its wings.

'Bloody hell!' the man exclaimed furiously. 'Damnation to that wretched machine! Damnation to Jeff for hotfooting it back before I could throw you in. Damnation most of all to you!' He glowered down on her.

Jessica lowered her gaze to the tarmac and waited wisely for the first of his fury to diminish. After a few moments she said: 'What now, Mr— Tim?'

'The name is Fortescue,' he said more coolly. 'Tim Fortescue. From the little I've gathered from your fantastic story you were expecting a Tim Browning.'

'It's not fantasy, Mr Fortescue,' Jessica defended, 'and I only knew of a Tim.'

'Old Tim Browning is out at Falling Star, not here.'

'Is Falling Star a subsidiary?'

'Yes.'

'Then why all the fuss?' Jessica queried. 'I can quietly slip out of your life and join my brother there.'

He took off his ten-gallon hat, then replaced it further down his forehead. 'And how,' he asked drily, 'do you propose to do that?'

'Perhaps you can loan me a car,' Jessica suggested timidly.

'No.'

'A bike.'

'No.'

'I could walk,' she tried.

'Two hundred kilometres?'

'Two—— Is it that far?' Jessica stared up at him.

'Much further, actually,' he shrugged, 'but for everyone's convenience I had the Falling Star home and offices moved nearer to S.D. The Star adjoins S.D.'s former northern boundary, Morning Star touches the old S.D. southern end. I bought out both stations at the last bad cattle plunge five years ago.'

'Easy for you then to play tough.' Jessica could not resist that. 'Easy for one of the lucky fellows.'

There was a silence, and, regretting her words, she ventured a nervous look at him. He stared stonily back at her, no blue showing at all this time, only angry, dark slits. She waited apprehensively, but he said nothing, except——

'Get in.'

'Get in?' she queried.

'Get in the waggon, Miss Makin.'

'What about my bags?' Jessica asked.

He went across, took them up, then fairly threw them in the back of the car.

'Get in yourself,' he said.

Jessica did.

He sparked the engine, then released the brake. They left the field and started along a straight, narrow road in the direction of the huddle of buildings.

Jessica was wondering to which of the collection he was taking her when abruptly he changed direction. The small fork he followed was not even a track, merely a faint ground indication that someone sometimes passed over here.

'Johann,' Tim Fortescue said shortly and cryptically.

'He is?' Jessica asked.

'My paymaster.' For a moment the blue eyes

beneath the forward-tilted hat left the winding
way and held her eyes. They challenged her, but
this time Jessica did not try to tell him that her
brother was that.

Instead she asked: 'Doesn't this Johann live in
the—in the——' She sought for a right word,
then came out triumphantly: 'Doesn't he live in
the beef machine?'

One brow lifted sardonically at her tag, but
Tim Fortescue made no comment.

'Johann comes from Austria, and, like the
other Johann, he has a leaning to Viennese
waltzes.'

'Strauss,' murmured Jessica. 'But why would
leaning to Viennese waltzes bar him from the——'
She hesitated.

'From the beef machine,' Tim Fortescue
finished for her. 'It doesn't. The fellows quite
liked his gentle classics, but Johann couldn't take
their Western music. It was all quite amicable.
Johann moved out to an old droving shack, and
he commutes to your so-called machine on a bike.
Hence the ill-marked path.' He nodded to the
track.

'Why are you taking me to this Johann?' Jessica
demanded. 'Is it to prove to me your paymaster is
not my brother?'

'I know it's not your brother.'

'Then?'

'I want to find out if there actually is a
brother,' Tim Fortescue shrugged, 'or if you're
only trying to put a Sydney swifty over me.'

'I come from that city, and I've never heard of

a Sydney swifty,' Jessica said coldly.

'Not heard—but dealt?' he insinuated. 'You said yourself you'd only been existing from day to day, so how much more pleasant to prise your way in here and live on the fat of the land. Beef fat.'

'You're abominable!' Jessica snapped furiously.

'Yet dead on?' he probed.

'Not dead on,' she contradicted. 'How, if I had no brother here, would I ever have heard of you?'

'They say a wind will carry a message of gold,' he came back, 'so I have no doubt a message about a beef baron could be blown along, too.' He took his eyes off the track a second time to look hard at her.

'Beef baron!' Jessica scorned.

For reply he told her laconically that his three holdings added together comprised a sixth of the entire Centre. 'I would be quite a catch,' he concluded.

'You a catch!' she scorned.

'For someone existing from day to day,' he reminded her evilly. He grinned.

'You can't mean me?' Jessica protested incredulously.

He pretended to look around him. 'I don't see anyone else here, Jessie.'

'I'm Jessica Makin.'

'I don't see anyone else.'

'You—you preposterous, swollen-headed, country lump!' Jessica burst out. 'As though I'd— I'd—— Why, you would be the last man in the world for me!'

'But you would still settle for me if I were that last, wouldn't you? Women are like that. They have to have a male.'

'Not always, and not me.'

'We'll see.' Again that edged grin.

'See what?' Jessica gritted. This man was impossible! she thought.

'I could say we'll see how it turns out in the end, and whether you do or not.'

'Whether I settle on you?' She looked at him in disbelief.

'Yes, Miss Makin.'

'Well, I can tell you now I won't.'

He shrugged carelessly. 'Or I could say,' he changed, 'that we'll find Johann and hear his report. As well as being paymaster, Johann is the personnel man. He'll know at once if there's a Makin.'

'After which?' Jessica enquired.

'We'll see,' he replied maddeningly again.

They began twisting through low eucalypt and high Mitchell grass, and some of Jessica's desolation must have reached the man, for he said thinly: 'Don't trip over your bottom lip when you get out, it's not that bad.'

'This country?' Jessica asked.

'Yes,' he said.

'Sixty thousand branded cattle and one thousand horses is to me.'

'I see Jeff has been talking. Well, what was it you wanted, then?'

'I wanted a home away from home,' Jessica admitted. 'Welcome.'

'And instead you get a beef machine.' He laughed. 'Not to worry,' he advised, 'I'll get you out of here. By heaven, I wouldn't think of doing anything else. And yet . . .' His voice stopped sharply, rather the same as he had stopped earlier. Again his face was thoughtful. But this time he did not say what he was thinking, he drove on until a rough shack appeared before them in the olive-green bush. There was actually a small garden around it, and a bike was propped against a wall. *The Blue Danube* drifted tantalisingly out on the hot still air.

Tim Fortescue cut the engine, put a barbarian finger on the horn, and left it there. Presently the music halted, and a grey-haired man came to the door. Only then did the finger leave the horn and Tim Fortescue leave the car.

'Hi, Johann.' There was no apology for breaking into the music. 'I have a query for you. Is there a Makin in our outfit?'

'Yes, boss—Toby Makin. He's at Falling Star. He does their accounts. He's a good boy, and doing very well.' Johann answered promptly and amicably; he did not seem at all put out at having his after-work music so rudely interrupted.

The Austrian was looking at Jessica now, looking with all the old European gallantry he had obviously been reared to.

'If I am not mistaken this young lady would be his sister,' Johann bowed.

On an impulse Jessica got out of the waggon and extended her hand, and the man took and kissed it. Across his bowed head as he did so Jes-

sica's eyes met Tim Fortescue's. They flicked
impertinently at her.

'That's all I want to know, Johann,' Tim
nodded. 'Go back to old Vienna.' He indicated
the door of the shack, and Johann smiled, bowed
once more to Jessica, then went inside again. At
once the strains of *The Gipsy Baron* enfolded
them, but the alien sweetness was lost for Jessica
as once more she was ordered sharply:

'Get in.'

Tim Fortescue drove silently for several
minutes along the ill-marked track back, then
suddenly, with no warning at all, he halted the
waggon with a rough jerk, then he turned round
to Jessica and took her hand in his.

Within moments she was in his arms.

CHAPTER TWO

IT was all so unexpected, so unwanted and so outrageous, that for a few stunned moments Jessica did nothing at all, she simply remained in his arms. Then her vision cleared, her senses returned, her indignation recovered from its numbed state, and she began to struggle, kick and scratch.

Tim Fortescue released her with unflattering alacrity, making a worse farce of the performance, if such was possible. As he did so he drawled: 'Nothing dastardly intended, Jessie Makin, it just seemed a quicker way of telling you than coming eventually to the point. Cattlemen have to do that, they know they have to act fast if they're to get the job done.'

'I,' retorted Jessica furiously, 'am not cattle!'

'No,' he agreed drily, 'I rather gathered that fact just now.'

She made as if to turn on him again, but he anchored her before she could do so with a quick return of a muscular, brown arm.

'At least give me a hearing,' he requested.

'After that unwelcome approach?' she disbelieved.

'Actually it was unwelcome for me, too,' he submitted, 'and I suppose I shouldn't have done it, but at the moment it seemed a short cut.'

'What short cut?' Jessica demanded.

'A short cut to the personal relationship I've decided to establish between us, Miss Makin. You and I are about to announce an engagement.'

'Whose engagement?' Jessica squeaked.

As he had before, he pretended to look around him.

'I don't see anyone else here, Jessie,' he said once more.

'You—you——' But words eluded her.

Impatiently he dismissed her bleat. 'Yes, I know all that, and in a way I understand, but frankly there isn't much time.'

'Time?' echoed Jessica. 'Mr Fortescue, what is all this? And remove your hand at once!'

He complied, telling her as he did that the idea had occurred to him on their way to Johann's shack.

'I was promising you I would get you away from S.D.,' he reminded, 'assuring you that I wouldn't think of anything else . . . and then the idea struck.'

'I wish it had,' Jessica came in, 'I wish it had concussed you! Then we wouldn't be talking this gibberish.'

'Except that it isn't,' he answered. 'It could, if carefully, convincingly played, be my way out.'

'Way out of what?' Jessica demanded.

'A position I'm in, a position I don't like at all, a position I won't have. My God, never underestimate the power of a woman!'

'A woman in this womanless place?'

'Two of them.' His bottom lip shot out.

'You're not trying to tell me that you, the mighty beef baron, can't take care of two women?' Jessica sneered.

'I could, if I was brutal, but it just happens that I'm not.'

'That I can't believe,' Jessica said with feeling, and she rubbed the arm where his fingers had anchored.

'Sorry,' he said indifferently, his attention still on himself, 'I can see now that that was a mistake.'

'It was,' Jessica snapped.

'I can see I should have explained,' he continued. 'I shall now.'

'No, thank you, I'm not interested,' Jessica rebuffed.

'All the same I'm going to,' he ignored, 'and all the same you are going to listen.' A pause. 'After which, all the same you are going to agree.'

'Agree to what?'

'Our apparent engagement,' he replied.

'No way, Mr Fortescue, now or ever.' Jessica gave a contemptuous laugh.

'Nonetheless you will do as I say,' he warned her, 'otherwise——'

'Otherwise?' she asked.

In reply he leaned across her and opened her door.

'Otherwise I'll shove you out,' he said quite coolly, 'and you can take over from that point.'

'Take over to where?' she asked incredulously.

'Wherever you like. It won't concern me. You could go back to Johann, I suppose, but I hardly think that hand-kissing and Strauss would be your cup of tea for very long. Besides' . . . not permitting an indignant interruption . . . 'there's only one bed there, which undoubtedly the good Johann, coming from the old gallant school, would give to you, sleeping on the floor himself.' A pause. 'On the other hand perhaps you both——' A deliberate and maddening look.

'You're impossible!' Jessica burst out.

'So is the outback scrub at night,' he warned, 'no velvet moss here to lie on, only gibber and prickles.' He nodded, and she looked beyond the waggon and saw that late afternoon was creeping in, the olive growing less green and more grey, shadows beginning. Involuntarily she shivered.

'You wouldn't do it,' she challenged.

'Don't try me,' he advised.

'Why can't I go over to Toby?' she appealed. 'Get out of your hair?'

'Because suddenly I've decided I need you in my hair to get rid of them.'

'Get rid of the women?'

'Yes.'

'After which you'll get rid of me?'

'Of course. I want you as much as I want them. As for Falling Star, it's right out. We've been asked by the Government to conserve energy, and S.D.'s contribution is a once-monthly branch inspection instead of every week. Since this month's was only yesterday, you have four more weeks less one day before you can go across. In other words, Miss Makin, it's either Johann, the bush—or me. *Now* will you hear me out?'

'Yes,' Jessica sighed.

He took out the makings of a cigarette and packed and rolled it. His movements were slow and deliberate, and Jessica suspected he was doing it more to think than to smoke. This must have been true, for after he had licked the edges of the thin paper together, looking enigmatically at her as he did so, he put the cigarette in a case.

'Back in the Saffron Downs homestead,' he explained, 'to which I now propose to take you, are two women. One is my elderly godmother, the other is a would-be wife.'

'Your would-be wife?' Jessica asked.

He gave her a withering look, but still nodded.

'Mainly the intention springs from Phyllida, my godmother, but young Gillian could be interested, too. After all, I'm not exactly a monstrosity, am I? After all, I'm——'

'Quite a catch,' Jessica finished for him.

Quite blatantly he agreed.

'It's the good catch angle that had brought Godmother Phyllida hotfooting it up here with her personal idea of a suitable wife,' he said. 'That's a little unfair of me, I suppose, old Phyl does love me. However, this Gillian, who's Phyl's great-niece, is obviously much loved, too. So what better idea' . . . he spread his big brown hands . . . 'than bringing two loved ones together?'

'Except,' Jessica inserted, 'that you don't want it?'

'Add to that that I won't have it,' he told her,

and again he stuck out his bottom lip.

They were both silent for a while.

'It all seems quite simple to me,' Jessica said presently. 'You just say No. After all, you seem to have no trouble yelling No at me.'

'You're not Phyllida,' he groaned.

'She can't be that bad!'

'She's worse. You see, I happen to like the old pest, and therein lies the trouble. Phyllida was wonderful to me in my school years, something I'll never forget. There's no greater trauma for an outback boy than suddenly to be confined to a city classroom, dormitory, quadrangle. But for Godmother Phyllida I would never have made it to matriculation, something my father wanted very much. I was hopelessly homesick, but Phyl saw me through. She took me over every weekend. She made life possible, even, at times, moderately enjoyable.' He shrugged.

There was another silence. During it Tim Fortescue looked challengingly at Jessica, eyes dark slits again, and she knew he was waiting to answer what she undoubtedly would ask.

Since it was expected of her, she asked it.

'Your mother had died?'

'No.' His reply was unadorned and harsh. 'No,' he said forcibly again.

'To make it worse,' he went on, 'the same thing had happened to my father. His mother had also left her husband. It appears that the Fortescue wives had a talent for not bringing up their young.'

'Perhaps they were not encouraged to,' Jessica

dared.

'Should motherhood need encouragement?' he flashed.

'Out here I consider it might need help—and love.'

'Well, my father got no help or love from his mother, and I got the same from mine. So' . . . a hunch of his big shoulders . . . 'it stops at that.'

'You mean stops at no more Fortescue children?' Jessica interpreted.

'No, stops at no more Fortescue wives. In spite of my godmother, one female I do care about, I am not marrying her Gillian. And you, Jessie Makin, are going to aid and abet me in that.'

'Oh, no, I won't,' Jessica said at once.

'Then get out.' He nodded to the open car door. 'Walk back and ask Johann to shelter you until such time as you can save money to fly home, because you're not flying free, not on my Cessna, Miss Makin. Also, don't go getting any ideas that failing Johann one of the other men will take pity on a pretty face. They're all of the same mind as I am.'

'A community of woman-haters?'

'No, woman *victims*. Every man here, save Johann, has a bitter story to tell.'

'You wring my heart,' Jessica said contemptuously. 'S.D. should be B.S.—broken souls.'

'At least men have souls,' he flung. 'No, the men are normal males, and in time they get back in the social whirl again. But here they can lick their wounds as they work.'

'A touching story.' Jessica pretended to gulp.

'I'll go back to Johann,' she decided. 'I'll ask to use his phone and I'll give Toby a ring.'

'There's only one place in this outfit from which to ring, and that's the homestead.'

'Where you won't permit me to do so,' Jessica supposed.

'You'll be allowed,' he said coldly, 'but it will avail you nothing. You heard Johann say when I asked him about a Toby Makin that Makin was a good boy and doing very well. Well, what reception do you expect from a good boy doing well? From a faithful employee?'

'Also a brother,' Jessica reminded him.

'It won't be what you want,' Tim Fortescue warned her, 'you'll be bawled out for making a fool of him, and so you should.' He stopped a moment to let that sink in.

'No, Jessie Makin,' he went on, 'there's only one way out of this, and here it is: You met me in Sydney . . . fortunately I was down there recently . . . and one night our eyes met.'

'What?'

'Our eyes met across a crowded room . . . the rest of the song. But I had to get back again, so what happens? This afternoon I go out for the mail and find you.'

'You mean—you mean I followed you up here?' Jessica gasped.

'Yes. Of course we'd been exchanging a letter or so.'

'. . . Love letters?'

'Well, they weren't bills,' he grinned.

'You're quite crazy!' said Jessica after a fuming

minute.

'Perhaps I am, but only something like this, someone like you, will rid me of Phyllida and the would-be wife. Also' . . . a reminding sidelong look . . . 'put *you* on your feet again.'

'What do you mean?' she demanded.

'Isn't it obvious?' he asked. 'I will pay you ——' He named a sum that made Jessica blink.

'Also, as of course you already know, it would be an *apparent* engagement—no strings, nothing at all. Heaven knows, an involvement is the last thing I want.'

'You're a rat,' Jessica told him.

'A hunted rat just now, hunted by two females. But I'm not going to be caught.'

'Then tell the women that,' said Jessica, exasperated, 'be a man and tell them no, no and no.'

'Oh, I'm a man,' he returned drily.

'Then tell.'

'I have told,' he groaned. 'I've told them in every way a gentleman can—and no sneers from you as to my being a gentleman, Miss Makin. I've reached the end of my tether. My fund of evasions and subtleties has dried up. Short of force I can only resort to this.' Deliberately he turned and took her in his arms.

He did not hold her, though, he released her at once. 'That was just to demonstrate,' he said, 'to show my intention. With luck we might not even have to reach a stage of engagement. My godmother may see the light, pack up and go.'

'With Gillian?'

'My God, yes, with Gillian. That's what this is

all about. All that might be required is for you to look fondly at me at times, perhaps prepare a special favourite dish . . . if Alf will permit you . . . put on a proprietorial air as you glance around the place.'

'Go on,' said Jessica, fascinated.

'A touch of your hand when they're watching,' he said. 'A stolen kiss.'

'Oh, no!' she refused.

'Not at once, if you think so. I'll leave the build-up to you. Just so long as they get the message, and go.'

'After which I can go?' she asked.

'Go either to Falling Star, or back to Sydney. With a fat cheque in your hot hand you should get a much better flat. But——'

'But?' Jessica asked.

'It has to begin at once. No mulling over it. Already my godmother is altering the furniture, planning curtains. You will return with me now. I'll explain how you arrived with the mail, and how you'll be staying. As I explain, you will be looking at me.'

'Across a crowded room,' Jessica inserted.

'I see you have the idea,' he applauded, and put a rewarding hand on her, which she promptly brushed off.

'Bad marks for that,' he told her.

'We haven't started yet,' she said.

'Meaning you *will* start, Jessie Makin?'

'The name is Jessica.'

'I'll call you Jessie. It will sound cosier.' He smiled at her.

Jessica did not smile back. She could not. But she knew she was not in any position to refuse him. To get out of this hateful place she had to go along with him. With that in mind, she answered: 'Very well, Tim Fortescue, I agree.'

He started the waggon again, then proceeded through the high Mitchell grass and the low spinifex, and pretended not to hear her audible:

'What else can I do?'

As they made their way along the barely defined track to the fork he told her a little about S.D.

'It was named Saffron Downs for obvious reasons.' He nodded his head to the miles of yellow-gold terrain. 'I have mainly Santa Getrudis cattle, and that means very good herds, in short Grade I. There's a lot more to it than what the movies give you, it's not all overlanding or road trains, it's dipping, T.B. testing, horn-trimming. There have to be regular dips for tick and buffalo fly. There's cutting out needed beasts ... that's called drafting. I have aerial mustering now, and aerial bore inspection. I have my own power, saddle maker, grader, even a picture show.'

'Have you a clinic?' Jessica asked.

'There's a resident vet.'

'I meant for the humans.'

'The Flying Doctor sees to them. Most of the complaints are "done in" backs. There are so many busted backs in the Centre and the Territory through riding accidents an orthopaedic man could have a ball.'

They reached the fork, and Tim Fortescue

turned the waggon in the direction of the large huddle of buildings that had so frightened Jessica. Silently she noted the names on the buildings as they passed them: Quantity Surveyor, Quality Research, Facilities Officer, Supply Depository, the ever-popular Store and Canteen . . . in all a very varied community of woman-haters, she thought.

She was not aware that her lip had dropped until Tim Fortescue said with amusement: 'What did you expect? A row of little cottages all named Emoh Ruo?'

'Is that the name of your house?' she asked.

'No name yet. I'm leaving that choice to my future wife, name of Jessie Makin. No, don't look like that, Miss Makin, this is for real now, we've reached your place of work, the job has begun.' He waved ahead.

Jessica looked at a typical Australian outback house, as wide as it was long, surrounded by verandahs on all sides, making it look like a schoolgirl's regulation hat.

Tim pulled up the waggon, then turned and regarded her. She saw that once more his blue eyes were enigmatical slits.

'Welcome to your new home,' he said. Then he added: 'Wife.'

CHAPTER THREE

TIM Fortescue preceded Jessica to the front verandah. Through the wide-flung, double entrance doors she could see a long, straight hall, faithful to the design still favoured in colonial homesteads. There was the traditional geometrical arrangement of rooms on either side of the hall, a considerable number of rooms in this instance, making it a large family house.

Without a family, Jessica thought.

'They'll probably be outside,' said Tim, and he moved round, Jessica following him, to the next side of the house. When this verandah proved womanless, he moved to the third, and there he stopped and nodded. Sitting under a large sunshade were two women, an old woman, a young woman. The older lady was sewing, the younger one turning over the pages of a magazine.

For a moment Jessica studied them. The senior ... no doubt Godmother Phyllida ... was well preserved. The junior ... called Gillian, Jessica recalled ... was pretty. The girl had the soft flower look that her brother would have appreciated, Jessica's mind ran on, but she was not aware that she had murmured this aloud until Tim Fortescue said drily:

'Then if you fail, we'll try Falling Star, foist Gillian on your brother.'

The sound of his voice if not his words must have reached the pair under the umbrella. They looked up, and Jessica saw that Tim's godmother was *very* presentable, Gillian *very* pretty. But more than that she registered that they were both *very* surprised.

Gillian's eyes were widely opened, but in Phyllida's case it was her mouth. The old lady was utterly amazed, and close up her amazement appeared unmistakable dismay.

'Why, Timothy——' she began.

Tim Fortescue came forward and kissed his godmother.

'Presenting Miss Makin,' he introduced. 'Godmother dear, this is Jessica ... Jessie to me.' When he got to 'Jessie' he deliberately softened his voice, and Jessica inwardly squirmed. He turned and inclined his head to the pretty girl. 'Jessica and Gillian,' he said.

There were murmurs all round, and then a silence. The old lady broke it with all the characteristic good manners of her years.

'How do you do, Miss Makin,' she said politely. 'Will you take tea?' But even her genteel upbringing could not prevent her from flashing her godson a look and reproving: 'Really, Timothy, you are the limit!'

'Yes, pet,' Tim Fortescue agreed cheerfully, 'and we'll have tea. But inside. It's too hot here.'

He led the way into the house.

It was a very sparse interior, Jessica found, the meagreness of undemanding male usage. There was barely an article that was not basic, and certainly no softening touch. An attempt had been made, presumably by the women, Jessica thought, to make it more agreeable, but the jar of flowers and the makeshift curtains did little except prompt a snort from the unimpressed owner. He mumbled something that sounded like 'Clutter', then strode out to the hall and shouted: 'Are you there, Alf? Bung on the billy.'

'Gillian has gone to the kitchen already, Timothy,' Godmother Phyllida shuddered. She turned from her godson to Jessica. 'When did you arrive, Miss Makin? How did you come? Are you tired?'

'She came along with the mail, Godmother,' said Tim. He handed the old lady her letters. 'Therefore,' he went on, 'she flew. No, she's not tired, are you, Jessie?'

'No,' Jessica had to agree.

The sound of a creaking tea-waggon prevented any more niceties. Gillian pushed the protesting contraption, probably protesting from long lack of exercise, and behind her came a plainly worried man wearing a large cooking apron.

Godmother Phyllis looked at him with distaste and implored her godson to tell him to go. 'We can manage quite well without him,' she complained.

'Well, *I* can't, after *you* leave,' said Tim.

This silenced her, and while she thought of something else Tim put his hand on the man's shoulder and said quietly: 'Later, Alf.'

Mollified, if not satisfied, Alf went.

Phyllida had found her tongue. She said: 'He's

very rude, Timothy.'

'So would you be if you were being usurped. I told you before to keep out of his domain.'

'Domain!' Phyllida closed her eyes in disgust. 'Like the rest of the house the kitchen is quite impossible. A place has to be lived in to—to——'

'This place is lived in,' Tim said.

'I mean lived in by a normal family to become a real house, become a real home.'

'I'm sure you're right, dear,' Tim placated. 'Now open your mouth and I'll silence you with cake.' He held a plate under Phyllida's nose. He took a piece himself and began to munch, then, as Phyllida remarked that dear Gillian had made it, he put it to one side. It was a silly thing to do, Jessica thought, but sillier still, and far too apparent, was his following enthusiastic statement that Jessie, too, baked cakes.

'How nice,' said his godmother flatly, not looking at Jessica, who was looking surprised at this news, since in a flat shared by four, you were lucky even to find space to boil an egg.

'So you came with the mail?' Godmother Phyllida asked Jessica, but still not looking at her.

'Yes,' said Jessica.

'It was a lovely surprise,' Tim glowed. 'I hadn't expected her.'

Jessica, not liking the position of designing female that he had put her in, inserted: 'Of course there'd been an exchange of letters.'

'Yes ... letters.' Tim Fortescue let his voice trail off.

There was silence all round for several moments, and during it Gillian got up and replenished the cups.

'How long is Miss Makin intending to——' Phyllida began.

'How long is Jessie staying?' asked Tim. 'As long as I can persuade her, yet no doubt she'll disappoint me and leave after you two go.'

There was another silence, and again Gillian rallied.

'I think I'd better fix up a room for Jessie,' she offered.

'Jessica,' appealed Jessica. 'Can I help?'

She got up after the girl and followed her out to the hall.

Gillian selected a bedroom to the left. 'This is the east,' she explained. 'The morning sun is quite pleasant, but the western aspect can be very savage in the afternoon. We all sleep on the east.' She opened a closed door.

She left Jessica standing there while she went to collect linen, and Jessica looked around her.

The room was adequately furnished but very dated. The bed, dressing table and wardrobe were the old embellished type much in favour four decades ago.

'If Tim keeps these pieces a few years longer,' Gillian remarked, coming back with sheets and blankets, 'they'll be in demand as antiques.'

Jessica liked them, she also liked the honeycomb quilt that Gillian had brought. She got to the other side of the bed and together they made it up.

'I feel dreadful imposing on you like this,' Jessica ventured. She felt that something had to be said.

'It's Tim's house, and he wanted you, so how could it be an imposition?' Gillian pointed out.

'It could be one on others. On—you.'

'Not at all,' Gillian assured her for herself, and she sounded sincere.

'But still unexpected?' Jessica persisted.

'Yes,' Gillian agreed, 'you were that.' But she still gave Jessica a friendly smile.

She plumped a pillow and asked Jessica if this was her first visit to the Centre.

Jessica nodded, and Gillian said:

'It's mine, too. Do you think you'll like it?'

'I've barely arrived.'

'It's said that the Inside is country you like, or don't like, at once.'

'I like it.' The words were out before Jessica knew it, and she was annoyed with her spontaneity. She yearned to say to this pretty young girl, obviously brought out for one especial reason, that her liking it did not mean that she was interested in becoming part of it, as that man outside, that wretched Tim Fortescue, was anxious to convey. She yearned to add that she was only interested in getting *away*.

Gillian was adjusting an old-fashioned eiderdown cover, and she said tactfully: 'You and Tim . . .'

Irritated that Gillian should feel a need to use tact, Jessica said recklessly: 'No need to tread on eggs, Gillian, there's nothing between us.'

'. . . Not yet,' Gillian suggested, and she killed

a sigh.

Jessica caught the sigh for all its short life, and said uncomfortably: 'I'm sorry, Gillian.'

Gillian answered simply: 'It was Aunt Phyllida's idea.'

'You mean coming here to—to——' Jessica's voice trailed off.

'To meet Aunt's godson? Yes.'

'Then you don't—you actually don't——'

'Don't like Tim?' helped out Gillian. 'Oh, no, I like him very much.' She had moved to the window, and Jessica, after a moment of hesitation, moved after her. Outside, some yards from the house, Tim Fortescue was unleashing a cattle dog, kneeling down to do it so not to put a strain on the dog's throat, and his big brown hands were astonishingly gentle on the rough blue coat.

'I mean,' Gillian murmured, her gaze on the length and breadth of the man, on the whipcord, muscular strength of him, the powerful physique, the distinct maleness, 'he's rather—well, wonderful, isn't he?'

'Is he?' Jessica mumbled thickly.

Gillian turned round on her, a little puzzled.

'Obviously Tim is attracted to you,' she told Jessica.

Jessica gnawed at her lip. What was she supposed to do now? she wondered.

'Perhaps he is attracted,' she said inadequately, 'I—I really don't know.' She looked appealingly at Gillian. 'Can we leave it at that for the moment?'

'Of course.' Gillian's assurance was warm and

sincere; she was a very nice girl, Jessica thought.
She put out her hand to her, and Gillian took it.

Presently Gillian confided: 'My mother died
last year, and my father died when I was only a
child, so now Aunt Phyllida is very anxious to
"place" me. I love Aunt, and I'm not opposed to
being "placed", I'm really a housewife sort of
person, I think, certainly never a career girl.'

'Feminine,' provided Jessica. 'The moment I
saw you I thought of my twin brother and how he
would have——' She smiled and stopped.

'Would have?' asked Gillian curiously.

'Would have liked you.' Jessica looked a little
apologetically at the girl. 'He goes for prettiness
like yours.'

Gillian blushed, and looked prettier than ever.
'Where is your brother?' she asked.

'He's up here. No, not right here, but at Falling Star.'

'Not Toby?' Gillian was delighted. 'I've met
Toby over the phone. It seems each time he's
rung Tim over some matter I've been around to
answer. He hasn't contacted Tim yet, poor boy.'

'Not poor,' corrected Jessica, and Gillian
blushed again.

'We've had some good talks,' she recounted,
'and a lot of laughs.' She paused. 'So Toby is
your twin.'

'Yes, indeed, and if I don't immediately tell him
I'm here he'll learn it from another source,
and bawl me out.' Bawl had been Tim Fortescue's description, Jessica thought. Mr—I
mean Tim said all the phone calls had to go from

here.'

'That's right,' confirmed Gillian. 'There are lines to the different S.D. sections, but this is the receiving and distributing department. The phone is down the hall, an old-fashioned model on the wall. Tim has never altered it. You'll see the call signs by the receiver. You'll dial Falling Star.'

'I hope Toby is there.'

'He will be. Falling Star is small, only one other person, besides old Tim Browning, the subsidiary boss, in the office. Oh yes, you'll get Toby.'

Jessica nodded, left the bedroom and went down the hall. She had a little trouble at first with the line, Gillian standing around ready to help her. When she did get through Gillian turned tactfully to go, but before she could do so Toby came very vociferously and very angrily over the wire.

'I was about to buzz you, you impossible fool of a female!' he shouted. 'What in Betsy are you doing up here? You should have written me first, asked for permission—can't you see the rotten position you've put me in?'

'How did you know I was here?' inserted Jessica with difficulty. 'Did *he* ring?'

'No, *he* did not, if it's Tim Fortescue you mean. The pilot did. He wanted to know if you'd be coming to me. You certainly wasted no time there, did you?'

'Toby, listen, you've got it all wrong. I should have done what you say, but I acted impulsively.'

'As you always do, you clot. What will the big boss think of me having a sister like you? Of all the inane idiots you take the ruddy cake! Now listen to me, lame brain——'

'No!' Gillian had stepped forward to take the receiver from a now tearful Jessica. '*You* listen to *me*.' She had evidently heard every word. Jessica had no doubt that even Aunt Phyllida had heard from the drawing room.

'Who's that?' Toby's voice was quieter.

'The one you always get when you ring up,' said Gillian.

'Oh. Oh, I see.' Toby was much quieter now.

'I don't think you do, but *I* see. I see how telephone conversations can be deceptive, I see you're not at all what you try to sound. Also, if I had a brother who spoke to me like that I would disown him. Your sister has travelled all these miles to see you, and what do you do? Scream at her! I think—why, I think you're quite awful! So what have you got to say for yourself?' Gillian demanded furiously.

Now Toby's voice was so low only Gillian could have heard. After a while Jessica stopped trying to pick up a word here and there, saw by Gillian's face that things were smoothing over, so went back to the drawing room again. Here Tim's godmother smiled at her quite amiably.

'You have a brother at one of Timothy's off-shoots?' she asked. Obviously, as Jessica had thought, she had overheard.

'Yes,' nodded Jessica.

'You'll be going across?' the old lady asked

eagerly.

'Yes,' Jessica agreed.

'So nice for you, my dear.' Now everything was positively rosy. 'I wonder what that barbarian Alfred will give us for dinner.'

'It must be difficult catering out here,' Jessica commented.

'Not for a woman. A woman is imaginative, she improvises. All Alfred succeeds in offering is a large steak and a larger flat bread.

It sounded very attractive to Jessica, who hadn't eaten a steak for weeks.

'Timothy doesn't even notice, of course,' went on old Phyllida, 'he only understands cattlemen's food. I don't think Timothy realises how uncivilised he's become. Anyway, ever since we arrived here he's taken to eating in the canteen. Slip out to the kitchen, will you, my dear, and see if Alfred has started yet. Perhaps a new face around the place might give him flair.' Godmother Phyllida seemed to have forgotten her animosity; like Gillian, Jessica decided, she was intrinsically a nice person. Either that or the assumption that Jessica had come here to visit her brother not to take over her godson poured oil, if only temporary oil, on troubled waters. She positively beamed at Jessica as Jessica went to obey.

But Jessica's favoured position was to be very brief. In the hallway a hand caught her. It was Tim Fortescue's big hand, and in a moment she was out on the verandah.

It was dark by now. In the Centre, Jessica was to find, there was no elf light, no preliminary;

only brightness one moment, indigo black the next. In the deep plush of it the large brown hand went around her waist and stopped there.

But when the light snapped on in the drawing room, Tim deliberately drew Jessica into the glow of it, and then, forcing her into a position where old Phyllida could not fail to see her, he bent and kissed her. First her brow, then both her ears, then, tilting her chin up to him, her mouth.

He held that fourth kiss.

CHAPTER FOUR

DINNER was not steak after all, it was corned beef. Alf called it corned dog, causing God-mother Phyllida to close her eyes again, and he slapped it down with a large bottle of pickles and the inevitable flat bread.

'Now that's what I call a meal,' Tim appreciated, taking up a knife to carve the huge slab of meat.

His godmother did not answer, but it was not because of the 'dog', Jessica knew, it was because Tim was eating at home tonight and not at the canteen. There could only be one reason, the old lady must be thinking. After that performance outside the drawing room it had to be *that* reason. Studiously Godmother avoided looking at Jessica.

It was not a pleasant meal, but that was not because of the distinctly un-fancy food, which privately Jessica found very welcome. You do not, she thought wryly, eat beans for months and then look askance at a plateful of beef. No, the reason was Tim Fortescue and his tiresome over-attention to his visitor. He was well mannered to all, but he fussed over only one person.

'Have another slice, Jessie.'

'Is it to your liking, Jessie?'

'Jessie, you must try this.'

Oh, shut up! Jessie screamed to herself.

Godmother Phyllida sat up stiff and correct, but, Jessica could see, Tim's behaviour was slowly but progressively crumpling her.

Gillian seemed unconcerned, ever since her telephone exchanges with Toby she had worn a small smile.

At last the meal was over, and the dishes taken out to Alfred. Now was the time, thought Jessica, for a boss to seek his men, to go over the day's affairs. But if Tim Fortescue generally did this, tonight he did not. He settled his ladies in the drawing room, then crossed to a radio player. Within minutes romantic music drifted out, nostalgic music. Significant music full of June, roses, moonlight and . . . looking deliberately at Jessica . . . eyes meeting across a crowded room.

Jessica clenched her hands and sat it out.

After an hour she knew she could not abide the pretence any longer. She got up, pleaded weariness, and said she would go to bed. Tim jumped up, too, and took her to the hall. Aloud he said: 'You know where everything is, don't you, Jessie?' *Not* aloud he hissed: 'Bad marks, Miss Makin, you should have lasted two more hours at least.'

'Heaven forbid!' muttered Jessica, and escaped him by going quickly to her room and closing the door. Even he could not open the door, not with Godmother Phyllida so near.

She undressed at once, put out the light, and got into bed. She did not go to sleep, though. Her whirling thoughts would not let her. The music stopped. The tea waggon creaked as evidently Gillian brought in some supper. Then Tim said he would turn in, and murmurs from the others indicated that they were ready, too. Presently the house was in darkness.

Almost at once there was a tap on Jessica's window. There was only one person who would tap, and the fool should have had enough sense at least to wait. Knowing the man's character by now, knowing he would not give up until she answered him, Jessica rose, put on a robe, and went to the window.

Yes, it was him, Tim Fortescue. His lips moved, and though, through the glass, she could not hear him, she could follow the progress of the lips.

'Open up,' they clearly said.

With a sigh she did so.

'I want to speak to you,' he told her after she had lifted the window.

'You're speaking, aren't you?' Jessica said crossly.

'I want to speak to you out here. No, don't go down the hall, you idiot, hop out of the window.' He leaned over and fairly hauled her across the sill.

'The row you're making you might as well have said what you wanted to say inside,' Jessica complained, 'if you think your godmother won't hear——'

'I want her to hear. That's what all this is about, remember? Also I want her to *see*, something she couldn't have done if you had remained in your room.'

'See what?' Jessica demanded.

'Us. Together.' He came a step closer.

'I hate to disappoint you,' Jessica told him wearily, 'but you did this act previously—in fact just before dinner.'

'And it had results,' he grinned evilly. 'Godmother was hurt.'

'But not mortally hurt,' Jessica reminded him. 'I'm sure she's recovered.'

'But not when she sees us this time, sees us slinking into the dark. Come on, woman, slink!' To her dismay Jessica was urged into the shadows. When they got there Tim Fortescue turned Jessica in the direction of the house. A light was on.

'See? Godmother's room,' said Tim with satisfaction.

At once the light went off, and Jessica sighed with relief.

'Now you've succeeded in whatever you set out to do may I now return?' she asked contemptuously.

'Not immediately,' he refused. 'I want Godmother to sweat it out a while, be beset with doubts. I want her to do that until she slips uneasily to sleep. Meanwhile I have a few complaints to make, Jessica. One: You didn't play your part very well tonight.'

'How could I?' objected Jessica. 'You monopolised the stage. Also, you were so corny about it, it sickened me. Kissing me in the sight of anyone at the window, for instance, when a genuine kisser would have sought out the dark.'

'Like this dark?' he interpreted, and kissed her again in the shadows, an entirely unemotional kiss, detached even, quite impersonal, almost a *tinge* of a kiss. Yet one, for some obscure reason, that oddly aroused Jessica ... aroused her by its very non-event, she supposed.

Annoyed at her inexplicable reaction to such a nothing, she added to her complaint: 'Also that sentimental music, all the hackneyed old songs!'

'They came from my heart,' he told her.

'You have no heart,' Jessica returned angrily. She was meaning the disappointed old lady, the uncertain young girl.

'I have. Give me your hand—feel it beat.' He had grabbed her hand, and forced it under his shirt. Before she could pull away, and it was not easy for his skin was damp and her fingers stuck to his flesh, he said: 'Have you a heart, too, Miss Makin?' and his other hand unfastened the neck of her gown, then the neck of her nightie, then went unerringly to her left breast.

'You have!' he acclaimed with wonder. 'It beats!'

'Leave me alone!' Jessica pulled away.

'Don't forget our agreement,' he reminded her.

'The agreement was only for such time as God-mother was around,' Jessica flashed back, 'and now she's not. The light is out. She's probably asleep.'

'Or watching behind the blind,' he suggested. 'But I do see your point. It's rather wasting our talents if we're *un*watched. Though not so fast'

. . . as Jessica, released now, turned to go back . . .
'I have more to say.'

'Yes?'

'Your brother rang me. He was full of apologies, quite abject, in fact.'

'Which would please you,' said Jessica.

'I was not unpleased, after all I am the boss. But what *dis*pleased me was how your brother learned you'd arrived. Jeff, my young pilot, rang him. Jeff wanted to know if you'd crossed over yet. He should have used his sense and known you couldn't be that quick, but he was too anxious to wait.' A pause. 'Wait for *you*. What went on during that hop?'

'Nothing, of course.'

'No "of course" about it—I fly myself, and I'm very conscious of blue skies turning to violet, of clouds like billowy balls. It's as romantic as eyes meeting across a room.'

'You're a fool!' Jessica snapped.

'But not the fool you would be if you two-timed me, Miss Makin. You're my girl first, and don't forget that.'

'You—why, you——' Words evaded Jessica.

'Just drop him before he starts,' said Tim with warning.

'Because of you?' she sneered.

'Yes, Jessie,' he advised.

'But it's only makebelieve, all a delusion.'

'Yet still in dead earnest—the purpose, I mean. To make the thing believable it has to be done properly. It may be a delusion, but it has to be a *dear delusion*. Follow me?'

'No.'

'Then practise,' he ordered, and before she could make an angry rejoinder he changed the theme.

'Do you ride?' he asked unexpectedly.

'Oh, yes.' Jessica said it confidently, she knew she rode well. Her twin was an excellent horseman, and his enthusiasm had fired her to learn, too, then to join a Sydney club. Toby's keenness had eventually urged him to the west, where, according to his contented letters, he had been able to do a lot of riding. Jessica, meanwhile, had had to get by with memories, because girls out of work can't afford to ride. Now, building up already on Tim's question, she found herself looking forward instead of at memories to a real, live horse.

'You sound very self-assured,' Tim Fortescue drawled. 'I didn't mean a merry-go-round horse.'

'I know exactly what you meant. I ride.'

'Good.' His evil smirk crept in again. 'Because Gillian doesn't. She hopes she does, but my God, she doesn't!'

'Meaning?' But Jessica had a horrible feeling she already knew what he meant.

'Meaning she's going to look a fool beside you, and that will depress her, discourage Godmother, delight me.'

'But not please me, so I won't ride.'

'You love riding. Your tone just said so.'

'But I don't love being mean,' Jessica said.

'That's strange, I had the impression you cultivated meanness,' he said blandly.

She ignored him. 'No, I won't be riding,' she declared.

'But you damn well will,' he came back. 'To-morrow morning I'm breaking in a few fellows I've selected. By fellows I mean horseflesh, both male and female, not humans. I'll announce this at breakfast, and I'll invite all you ladies to watch. After that we'll decide to do a little social riding ourselves.'

'Such intrigue!' marvelled Jessica. 'Couldn't you say a simple "Who's for a ride?"'

'Not for the result that I'm after. No, it has to be done subtly.'

'And nastily,' she inserted. 'You must be the nastiest man in the world!'

'I'll notch that on my belt.' Tim put his big thumbs in the embossed leather circling his firm, strong midriff. As an afterthought he said: 'You can notch meanness on yours, Jessie, but then you're not wearing a belt, are you? You're wearing a dangly thing to keep your dressing gown decent—what do they call them? Girdles.' He put out a hand.

Angrily Jessica went to brush the hand away, but his fingers caught hers.

'No hard leather belt,' he marvelled, 'just a soft silk rope round a soft silk girl.' His fingers began moving beneath the girdle.

'We're not on show now,' she said a little agitatedly.

'To my mind it's always good to keep in practice.' The hand kept moving.

Making a sudden move, Jessica escaped from

him. As she ran to the house she heard him swearing softly as he came after her. She clambered up the window but was unable to climb over before he reached her. Calmly he took her off the sill.

She was a little scared now, and began to kick at him.

'Calm down,' he advised. 'You were climbing into the wrong room, you were trying to get into my room, not your own. Come to think of it' . . . propping her on the correct sill . . . 'I should have let you carry on with that, it would have really clinched my case.

'Now get!' In case she didn't, he gave her a shove.

Eventually Jessica slept, but she did not feel as fresh as she should have in the morning. She had tossed around too long before oblivion finally had caught her. However, when she saw Gillian's pretty face over the breakfast table she knew that Gillian felt worse still. She saw that the girl was already guessing what might happen after the horse-break that Tim was talking about, that she was uneasy even at this stage, and her sympathy went out to her.

After the meal was over Tim suggested that the girls get into trews. 'Much more comfortable around the horse-break,' he explained. 'You as well, Godmother.'

'You know very well I never wear such things,' said Godmother Phyllida, and she was cross when he laughed hilariously. She was only mildly cross, though; she was obviously anticipating Gillian in the fetching jodhpurs she had purchased for her before they came to Saffron Downs. Gillian had a charming little figure.

In the end Godmother decided it was too hot to go, and the girls, both in jodhpurs, and Tim, wearing his riding breeches, set out. They did not take the waggon, it was not far, Tim said, and he could point out a few things that might interest them on the way.

There were many interesting things, but most of all, to Jessica, was the lagoon. It seemed strange to find a shimmering, silver-tinged little lake in this yellow-gold country, but there it lay, a stretch of sparkling water, insects weaving gauzy patterns above it, frogs singing a throaty chorus.

Not far round the lagoon rim the horses were gathered. At once Tim Fortescue stepped out and accepted a light crop from a stockman. He never used the whip.

Two of the jackeroos already had cut out the horses selected for the break, and from them Tim chose two fillies and a stallion to show the jacks, who were learning their job, what to do.

'Girls are touchy,' he said softly as he worked first on the grey filly, 'you need a lot of sympathy and a gentle touch. Stallions are different. They can be set in their ways. Always stand in front of a stallion with the noose wide open—use no deceit, they can see through that.' He dropped the loop cleanly over the stallion without any trouble.

Fascinated, impressed in spite of herself, Jessica watched the man with the second filly, a shining bay with a cream flash. Here, she thought, was a more spirited girl.

But once more Tim Fortescue spoke softly . . . yet this time there was an authoritative note in his voice.

Once his bright blue eyes met Jessica's, and she thought foolishly that although they were not meeting across a crowded room but across a breaking yard, the same arousal was there.

She stopped herself angrily. She was not aroused—never by him.

The blue eyes had narrowed. They seemed to be challenging her. See this filly, they seemed to be saying, I'm taming her. The bright blue eyes flicked at Jessica. *You* are the filly, the eyes said.

Jessica turned away.

The horse-break, Tim's part in it, anyway, was over. He handed the job to his head man, and sauntered across to the girls.

'After that,' he drawled, 'I'm sure you both feel like a ride. Do you ride?' He asked it with hateful innocence of Jessica.

'Yes,' said Jessica.

'And Gillian does,' he said quite kindly. 'Joe' . . . to a groom standing nearby . . . 'get out Rebel, Bluebell and Sam, will you?'

'Shall be done, boss.' Joe turned away.

About to accompany the girls, who were following Joe, Tim was asked a question by one of the stockmen. The girls waited a while, then trailed after the groom. Jessica could see that the unhappy Gillian was frankly anxious to get the wretched thing over. She walked beside her, wondering should she say something, deciding it might be better to let things pass.

Gillian never said a word.

When they got to the stables the three horses were tethered in readiness. Gillian hurried ahead to mount Bluebell before Joe could leg her up. She climbed clumsily, and Jessica felt desperately sorry for her. She was despising Tim for making the girl appear inept . . . when an idea struck her. Of the remaining mounts there was no need to be told who was Rebel and who was Sam. The lugubrious Sam was cropping peacefully, the larger, more spectacular Rebel tossing a silky mane. Jessica had no doubt that lugubrious Sam was intended for her.

'I'll make *him* the fool,' she thought.

She quickly mounted the bigger horse.

Immediately she realised she had made a horrible mistake, she saw that she had mounted her own *intended* mount, not his. For, in spite of Rebel's name, Rebel's looks, Rebel was clearly amenable . . . even meek. Tim Fortescue must have taken her assurance that she could ride with caution, for besides giving Gillian a gentle animal, he had allotted a gentle one to her. Jessica could have cried with mortification. If she had only gone to the other mount she could have paid him back a score.

In her pique she did something she had never done before. She pulled the horse's head sharply, then, of all things, she struck the shining flanks.

Tim's shout ... he had arrived on the scene now ... came at the same time as the horse's whinny of outrage. Too late Jessica realised that here was one of those vulnerable horses who will react only to love, never to physical discipline, who, once insulted, will give back what they got. Rebel rose on his back legs, gave another furious whicker, then set off, and certainly it was no amiable amble.

Starting with a brisk gallop, Rebel soon changed to an awesome bolt. Jessica had never dealt with anything like this in all her riding experience. She could hear Rebel's hooves digging in, and she never would have thought that on turf, even the rough turf of the Centre, hooves could make such a din. She had no time to wonder about it, though, she only had time to hang on. She must hang on, not because she did not want to look the fool that she had planned for Tim, but for her own health. Rebel literally was flying.

Then something streaked past her, a second horse, a smaller fellow. Why, it was Sam, lugubrious Sam whom she had thought had been chosen, out of caution, for her, but all the time, in spite of a lesser size, had been Tim's mount. Also Tim's very speedy mount, for Sam was easily outstripping Rebel.

'Pull up!' Tim's voice called authoritatively, and even in her absorption of trying to save herself, Jessica shivered at the tone.

'I can't!' she cried.

'Then stay on. I'm coming beside you. When I

shout "Clear", clear yourself and get ready to be hauled off. Have you got that?'

'Yes, but——'

'*Clear!*' He fairly rent the air with the order, and Jessica rid herself of the stirrups. The next moment she was being lifted bodily from Rebel, then deposited in front of Tim on Sam. A few moments later she was dropped unceremoniously to the ground.

Tim waited until the groom caught Rebel and towed him back to the stables, then he turned deliberately and flicked his whip at Jessica. He made it appear an accident, but he knew, and Jessica knew, that it was not. It barely touched her, but she looked up angrily.

'It's not what you should get,' he said in a low voice, 'and it's not where you should get it, but my God, Jessie, if you ever do that again, you *will* get it. You'll get the whole bit. Do you hear?'

'I hear,' Jessica mumbled.

'Then get back to the homestead and change your clothes—your pants are all marked. I only wish underneath the pants was marked. By Harry, and I could still do it!'

This time Jessica got moving. She did not walk back, she ran. Behind her, riding easily and lazily, came Tim Fortescue, temper over now, watching her painful progress, for she was sick, sore and sorry, with a small, edged grin.

At least, Jessica fumed, someone was amused.

CHAPTER FIVE

As well as Tim being quietly pleased with the affair, there were signs of hope in Godmother Phyllida. She took one look at Jessica's dishevelment and lost all her rancour. Compared to her immaculate Gillian, Jessica looked positively dirty, unkempt and not at all attractive.

'Run the bath, Timothy,' she ordered happily, 'make it hot and deep.'

'Very hot and very deep,' Tim agreed, 'and I hope the hot burns and the deep drowns.' But only Jessica heard him. Gillian was searching the medicine cabinet for emollient for bruises, Godmother was fetching towels.

'Give me a call when you're finished and I'll administer both the salve and the towels,' said Tim, still only for Jessica.

'You've administered enough!' she answered him furiously.

He looked at her narrowly. 'Don't underestimate me,' he warned, 'I haven't even started yet. Never forget this, Miss Makin—I, and I only, discipline my horses.'

'Also your women,' Jessica flashed.

'You're including yourself?' he flashed back, and Jessica wished she had not spoken.

He waited a while, then said: 'You're right, though—I, and I only, discipline my women.

However, good marks at least for playing the role
of my woman, for coming back chastened and
obedient for all, and Godmother, to see. Even
though I had to chastise you to get that result, I
thank you, Jessie.'

'You intended to chastise Gillian as well, didn't
you?' Jessica burst out. 'You intended to embar-
rass the poor girl by making her look inept. But
fortunately it didn't turn out that way.'

'*Un*fortunately for you,' he reminded her. 'Are
you still stinging?'

'No.'

'Then you will in the bath.'

He left it at that.

Jessica's sleep was sound that night, probably
because not only was she tired, but Godmother
insisted on giving her a sedative. Perhaps there
was another reason for the sedative, Jessica
thought, on the edge of slumber; perhaps it was
to assure Gillian her share of her godson, for
the last sound she heard as she slipped off was
Tim's and Gillian's laughter. So they were not on
such opposite sides as he tried to make out, she
thought.

When she went along to breakfast the next
morning, a little late, because the sedative certainly had worked, Tim had eaten earlier and
gone across to his office. Gillian said he would
not be back until lunch.

'But guess what?' she bubbled girlishly. 'Your
twin rang. He's coming across. I'm quite interested in meeting him. The telephone picture I get
could be quite wrong. I see him as fair, grey-eyed
and friendly.'

'He has a brown thatch, is pickle-eyed and a pill,' Jessica informed her. But the news that Toby was coming gave her an idea. Tim Fortescue had said she could not cross to Falling Star, but since Toby was coming anyway, there was no reason why she should not return with her brother.

No reason? Jessica had not taken account of the boss.

As soon as breakfast was over, Jessica, avoiding Godmother and Gillian, went unobtrusively out of the homestead and over the dry, yellow-gold grass to the administrative huddle.

She was intrigued as she passed the different 'shops' to see the smiles and the waves she received. For males who shunned females, the men were distinctly friendly.

She said this to Tim when she reached the managerial 'shop', and knocked and entered as the door said.

'They're not all abstainers,' Tim said drily. 'Some are up here to make money, for I pay highly. I demand good work and I give good wages. While the husband makes hay here, the wife is doing the same in a city office or factory. It all adds up to a cosy little house in the suburbs much sooner than they could ordinarily have afforded. What brings you here, Miss Makin?' he added. 'But good marks, anyway, for Godmother's lip will certainly drop when she knows you're chasing me.'

'I am not!' said Jessica indignantly. 'Also, she doesn't know.'

'Perhaps not yet, but I'll surely tell her. I'll say

'you did it for love. Yet I can't really think you crossed for love, Miss Makin, so what is it?'

'Toby. He's coming over from Falling Star. He rang, and Gillian took the message. I thought since you can't take the time off, or afford the petrol, to get me over to your subsidiary, I could go back with him.'

'No.'

'But if he's coming whether or not——'

'He's not coming. But many thanks for alerting me. I'll stop that little game before it even starts.' Tim took up the phone, and presently Gillian answered it.

'Tim here, Gillian,' Tim Fortescue said shortly. 'Get me Toby Makin of Falling Star. What? *What?*' Without another word, or any thanks, he slammed down the phone.

'He's already left,' he said. 'I'll have a piece of that young fellow! Also take that grin off your face, Miss Makin, because you're not leaving when he leaves. Why, you've barely started working out your agreement.'

'It would be better for you if I was right away,' pointed out Jessica diplomatically, 'then you'd need no agreement.'

'It would not be better. Don't get the idea that I want you around, because I don't. But I don't want those females around even more, so you have to stop until they go.'

'You can't make me,' Jessica persisted.

'Not bodily, perhaps—not, anyway, with everyone watching, but if you go, Toby goes, too.'

'Naturally.'

Tim Fortescue said: '*He goes for all time. I sack him.*'

Jessica stared incredulously at him. 'You wouldn't do that!' she appealed. 'He loves it out here.'

'Try me,' Tim said.

As she stood uncertainly there, Tim added: 'Now clear out—I have work to do. The moment your brother turns up, send him across. I have a few things to say to that fellow.'

Jessica left the office and crossed the yellow grass to the homestead again.

When she reached the big square house she saw a jeep drawn up, and when she reached the front doors she heard voices. Gillian's voice, Godmother's . . . and Toby's. Her twin was here. Jessica ran into the house.

They both always proclaimed a fierce brotherly and sisterly hate, but they both really loved each other, and they promptly embraced.

'You rat!' Jessica greeted Toby.

'Sister rat,' grinned Toby.

Godmother had asked Alf to make tea, and, surprise of surprises, Alf could make cakes. Not city cakes, but country brownie, cut and come again cake, currant rocks.

'Very nice, Alfred,' Godmother Phyllida commended, and, distinctly flattered, Alf went out in a glow—proving, Jessica thought, that not all the men at S.D. were immune to women.

Then she recalled one who was.

'Toby,' she reminded him, 'you're to report to

Mr Fortescue.'

'Of course,' Toby nodded, 'that's why I'm here. The big boss ordered Falling Star to bring across this report.' He held up a sheath of papers.

'Ordered?' Jessica disbelieved.

'Yes—by phone, last week. Why?'

Why indeed? Jessica gloated. Tim Fortescue might be the big boss, she was thinking gleefully, but he was a forgetful big boss as well. She sat back and enjoyed herself.

They were all doing that when Tim arrived for lunch.

Toby got to his feet at once, as he should for a superior, but when Tim Fortescue demanded: 'Why the hell are you over here?' and Toby reminded him, Tim was distinctly quiet.

Jessica glowed secretly at that, but Alf, bringing in the midday meal, was still in an outward glow from his cake success, from his praise, most of all, from Godmother Phyllida. Godmother, meanwhile, was in a very good mood. Undoubtedly Toby's unconcealed admiration of her niece was pleasing her, for certainly her godson never looked at Gillian like that.

Jessica could see that Toby could hardly take his eyes off the girl, so much so that it proved difficult later for Jessica to get a private word with her twin. But she did manage a brief exchange after lunch.

'Toby, I must go to Falling Star with you,' she pleaded.

'No go, Sis,' Toby answered. "You put me on the bad list coming here, but I'd be on the worse still list if I took you back with me.'

'Toby, I can't stay here.'

Toby answered a strange thing. He said: 'My
God, I wish I could!'

'What do you mean?' Jessica demanded.

'I can't tell you now,' Toby sighed, 'I have to
get going.'

'Take me, too, Toby,' she begged.

'And lose my job at S.D., possibly lose——'

'What?' Jessica asked again, but Toby had returned to the others.

'Goodbye, Mrs Reynolds,' said Toby, and he
went across and shook Godmother's hand.
'Goodbye, boss, I'll see to that detail you told
me. Goodbye, Sis.' A pause. '. . . Goodbye, Gillian,' and he left.

It was hours later . . . dark, dinner finished . . .
when he reappeared. They heard his country
boots clumping across the rough ground before
they heard his knock.

Tim answered the door and said: 'You! What
in hell has happened?'

'The jeep's ignition, I would say, boss,' Toby
groaned. 'I did everything I could think of, but it
was still no good. In the end I had to toss up
between here and Falling Star, and seeing that
here was miles closer——'

'How far had you got?' Tim broke in.

Toby answered, but Jessica could not hear
him, but it must have been a long way, because
Tim whistled and said: 'You must be tuckered.
Come in.'

There was no question of going out in the dark

to see the ailing jeep; it would have to wait till tomorrow.

Alf made some sandwiches for Toby, a pot of tea for everyone, and Gillian and Jessica, on Tim's advice, fixed up a bed.

'This should satisfy you, Godmother,' Tim could not resist teasing, 'a family home at last.'

Godmother Phyllida did not answer; she seemed a little uncertain about what was taking place.

The next morning Toby directed the S.D. mechanics to where he had left the jeep. He and Tim went with the mechanics, the plan being for Toby, after the repairs were finished, to proceed to Falling Star.

But an hour later they were all back at S.D., the repair truck towing the jeep. It needed major repairs, not running ones, and there was no facility at Falling Star for such a detailed job. Since there was no other jeep at the subsidiary, and since S.D. needed its own jeep, Toby would have to remain here until the job was done.

'How long will that take?' It was Gillian asking.

'All the morning, anyhow,' Toby said happily. 'It could even go into the afternoon.' He turned to Tim. 'What have you in mind for me, boss?'

'Nothing in your usual channel.' Tim shrugged, 'Johann won't let anyone near his books. You could give your sister a riding lesson, I suppose, she doesn't seem to have the knack.' He flicked Jessica a reminding look. 'However, I think I'll use you as a watcher on the mob that we're overlanding to the Lucy River—the beasts are resting on the western paddock before they take off, and if you go now you'll be just in time. Take the girls with you, they'll be interested, but for heaven's sake give them all the necessary gen. Here's the keys of the waggon.' Tim tossed them across.

When they got in beside Toby, Jessica asked curiously: 'What is this necessary gen?'

'It's the overlanders' text,' Toby told her. He quoted: '"Start no trouble and receive no trouble."' He added: 'There's some Brahma steer among this lot, and Brahma are touchy. If a wrong thing is done they can start a rush.'

'A stampede?' Gillian shuddered, and Toby nodded.

'What could be a wrong thing? Who would do it?' Jessica asked in her turn.

'Frankly, you and Gillian, as the onlookers, could,' Toby replied. 'The professionals are far too wary. You could speak too loudly, cough, even open a compact and shut it, and it could be on. It's all that delicate.' He looked sidewise at the girls. 'Understood?'

They nodded seriously because of Toby's serious face.

When they came to the cordoned herds Toby led them quickly up a small incline the better to see the spectacle, because it was indeed that. It was a copper day—that was the only description Jessica could think of. It was a bright, hard, deeper than gold day. She looked down and out.

As far as she could see was a press of cattle, a

great weaving mass of huge bodies and churning hooves. They were just in time, the mob was beginning its first move forward, and the dust as the beasts passed seemed wall-thick.

The native stockmen, conscious of their responsible position, wore their ten-gallon hats, high boots and bright shirts proudly. They were very professional, Jessica noted, even the slightest ripple in the sea of bodies where there should be no ripple sent them flying to the trouble spot, whips ready to crack, dogs on the alert.

They were so perfect that Jessica could not imagine anything ever happening . . . and yet it did.

Afterwards no one could say what actually started the short stampede, though Tim Fortescue shrugged and drawled: 'Even the flick of an eyelash can do it.'

The upheaval was over almost as soon as it began, the churning beast who started it back in the mob again, the press moving rhythmically.

But someone had been caught in the brief crush. Toby, who had left the girls further back, had been in the path of the sudden disturbance, and when the stockmen got things into order once more, Toby lay where he had been pushed down.

It was Gillian who reached him first, who knelt down and cradled his head in her lap.

Jessica came moments after.

'His pulse is all right,' Gillian reported tremulously. 'However, he's obviously concussed, Jessica, and I think, too, he could have injured a leg.

I can't find any wound yet, but I was watching him when the beasts closed in, and——' her voice cracked.

Jessica gave her a quick look. She herself had been watching the spectacle, but Gillian, on her own admission, had been watching—Toby. She, too, knelt down.

'He's losing blood.' Gillian indicated a spreading stain on Toby's breeches. 'We'll have to get him back at once.'

'Here's the boss drover,' Jessica reassured her, for Gillian was almost as pale as her brother. 'He'll tell us what to do.'

The stockman, after a quick, practised examination of Toby, put their fears to rest.

'He'll be all right.' Jessica noted that he said it to Gillian, not to Toby's sister. 'He's still breathing, and that's what counts. Between us' . . . he nodded to a couple of the drovers . . . 'we'll get him into the waggon. Can you manage after that?'

The two girls said Yes.

Carefully Toby was put in the back of the jeep, then, without asking Jessica, Gillian took up her position again. She cradled Toby's head in her lap.

After a moment's hesitation Jessica got behind the wheel. As she started the engine she heard the drovers' whips cracking once more, she saw the mob setting off.

Tim Fortescue was just leaving the homestead when they arrived back, and he was across to the waggon almost before they stopped.

'Hells bells, what's happened—— Oh, it's

young Makin.' Without a moment's hesitation he took out a pocket-knife and slit Toby's trousers where the blood now was spreading quite ominously.

'That's some gash,' he said when he had done so. 'I'll get the F.D.'

With more help Toby was carried inside, laid on a cot, made as comfortable as he could be made while they waited for advice.

The Flying Doctor was there in the hour, and, typical of men who have to make fast decisions, after stitching the gash he said: 'It's Base Hospital for this young fellow. I'll take him along with me.'

'Can't he be nursed here?' It was Gillian.

'Are you a nurse?' the doctor asked.

'No, but it's mainly rest that will be needed, isn't it?'

'Mainly,' nodded the doctor, 'but the injury could play up; a later concussion reaction is also quite likely. I feel he must be professionally watched. I'm sorry, Mrs Makin.'

'It's not Mrs Makin,' said Gillian. She glanced at Jessica. 'This is Miss Makin, the patient's sister.'

'And I'll go with Toby,' Jessica told the doctor. She felt she had been in the wings too long.

'It's not necessary,' the flying doctor declined politely, 'in fact you would be in the way. I have another case to pick up.'

'But——' began Jessica.

'You heard the doctor.' Tim had joined the

group round Toby. 'Do as he says.'

'But——' both the girls objected this time. To
no avail.

In minutes a stretcher was being wheeled in,
Toby being placed on it. Minutes after they
heard the whirr of the F.D.'s plane, and they
knew that Toby was being flown into the Base.

Godmother made a valiant effort to start a conversation, but no one seemed inclined to carry it
on. At last Gillian, very drawn, said she thought
she would lie down for a while, and as Godmother made a practice of resting it left only Tim
and Jessica, and Tim announced that he would
continue from where he had left off before Toby
was brought in, and that was back to his office to
finish the day's work.

It had to be now, decided Jessica, and she
stepped between him and the door.

'I *am* going, of course,' she told him.

'Going where?' He kept walking until he was
right up to Jessica. They almost touched.

'To the Base Hospital, or the nearest I can get
to it. After all, he is my brother.'

'So I've gathered, but he isn't dying, is he?'

'No, he isn't, but——'

'So there's no need for you to fuss.'

'I'm not fussing, and I think you must be the
most heartless man in the world to adopt an attitude like that!'

'On the contrary, I have a heart, and you know
it. You even put your hand on it to check its tick.'

'It ticked hate,' Jessica flung.

'It ticked what you wanted to hear, and I suppose you're entitled to that. But you're not entitled to leave here until you settle up, Miss Makin, so here you stay. Understand?'

'No,' snapped Jessica.

'You'll stay all the same,' he told her, and without another word he stepped back from her, and left the room. She heard him slam the door as he went.

CHAPTER SIX

TOBY did not progress as favourably as he should have. Initially there was a period of further concussion, and then the injury became infected and had to be watched closely.

Tim Fortescue was frequently in touch with the base hospital, and each time he would report formally to the patient's next of kin. That Gillian was there on each occasion was not surprising, for the two girls had become close friends.

Since Alf's surprising cake production, a friendship, too, had struck up between Godmother and Tim's cook. Godmother had decided to write an outback cookbook. Alf, flattered, excited at the prospect of having his name at the bottom of his bush recipes, disclosed all. As he had been a shearers' cook, a hydro project cook, a wheat, nickel and uranium cook, he had a fund of information to divulge, and Godmother, happily diverted, forgot her halfhearted animosity towards Jessica, forgot her over-protection of Gillian, and spent hours in Alf's kitchen, taking notes.

It was a busy period, too, for Tim, and he left the homestead early for the administrative huddle, skipped lunch, and came back late.

But he did provide a small car for the girls, a tough, rough little model, suitable for the tough, rough terrain.

'Only don't go too far,' he told them, 'it hasn't been overhauled lately, and I don't want you walking back like Toby had to.'

'Where can we go?' Jessica asked.

'Keep to the tracks and you'll find a few interesting items. There's some caves several kilometres out to the west, and there's a few wurlies around. You might even find some aboriginal carvings. This was once the old Mulya tribe's hunting ground, and there should be some evidence if you look around.'

The girls found the car stout and reliable, and enjoyed exploring the varied scene. After one got accustomed to the terrain the tracks seemed quite well defined, so instead of veering off along a wind indentation by mistake, as they did in the beginning, they stuck successfully to the flattened earth between the low eucalypt and the high Mitchell grass. In this way they never got lost.

They found the caves, they found the carvings, and to their delight on one occasion they found a wurlie. As well as being a sacred place, a wurlie could be an old aboriginal watering hole. This was a watering hole, and a very pretty one, deeply enclosed within an outcrop of rocks, so, because of its protection from the sun, a cool green instead of the usual sky-reflecting blue. It was also cold.

'Icy-cold!' warned Gillian, pulling her toes away and shivering.

But the day, like most of the Centre days, whether winter or summer, was warm, only the nights grew cool, and the sight and feel of water urged the girls to find somewhere to swim.

The lagoon would not be deep enough, it was only a place for dragonflies, gnats and frogs, then Gillian remembered hearing about an artesian pool not too many miles out.

'At least,' she said, 'it won't be like the wurlie, it will be warm.'

They found it the next day, a blue offering this time, blue also from the Salvation Jane growing around it as from the sky. They were happily floating in its balmy warmth when Tim Fortescue's waggon came fairly racing down to the pool's rim. Alarmed, thinking of things like crocodiles, which were not only unlikely but so far unknown around these parts, they heard later, the girls turned on their stomachs to swim to the bank.

Jessica made it, but Gillian did not. In turning she must have caught her foot in something that promptly entrapped her, then pulled her under, for only her hand, held up for help, now showed. Jessica at once made to cross to grab the hand, but she was grabbed herself, then pushed to one side. Tim Fortescue, evidently seeing the hand as she had, had plunged into the water. He was still dressed, but clothes did not impede him. Nor did they stop any of the impact of the shove away and the following rough push that he gave to Jessica.

'For pity's sake get yourself ashore!' he ordered furiously. 'I'll see to this one.' He dived under and brought Gillian up. She was spluttering and rather distressed, but she needed no resuscitation. He towed her to the bank.

'I'm sorry, Tim.' It was Gillian who proffered the apology; Jessica was too resentful—that shove and that push had been over-emphasised, she considered.

'So you should be,' Tim snapped. 'Nobody, but nobody, jumps into water without examining the situation first.'

'Crocs?' they both asked.

'No, not here. Anyway, it would only be a freshwater croc, and they're not man-eaters. They might bite off a limb or two to try the taste, but they'd spit it out again.' A grim laugh, but no one joined it.

'Why such a fuss, then?' It was Jessica, coldly.

'You didn't find anything alarming in seeing a hand sticking out of the water just now?' Tim demanded of Jessica. 'All these innocent-looking holes can have old logs in them, dead branches, weed traps, each making for entanglement, even death, for the unwary. I would advise you both to be more cautious in the future, except that I'm not doing anything so mild, I'm ordering you instead. Ordering you to stay away from waterholes. If you want to swim, the men have erected an above-ground pool near their quarters. If mixed bathing doesn't appeal, and it might not, since the prevailing dress is skin, pick your own time and tell them. Only no more holes, understand? Now I'm going home to change. Thanks to you two I'm soaked.' He got in the waggon without another word, reved the engine, and left.

'How did Tim know we were here?' asked Gillian after the dust of the departing waggon had settled.

'Eyes everywhere,' Jessica said acidly. 'A suspicious nature. A sense of wrongdoing even before it's done.' She helped Gillian gather their towels and magazines and together they climbed the bank back to their car.

'Well, swimming is out,' Jessica observed, touching the ignition, for it was her turn to drive.

'Yes.' But Gillian smiled faintly, and Jessica noted that she was not so annoyed as impressed. There was no resentment in her voice, there was even a tinge of a smile.

'He's all man, isn't he?' Gillian went on. 'These Centralians used to be called the all-the-way men . . . did you know that? . . . and certainly Tim is one.'

'Maybe.' But Jessica said it thoughtfully, not admiringly. She knew lots of women reacted favourably to mastery in a man, and she was now wondering if Tim was going the right offputting way with Gillian . . . that is if offputting was his real intent.

What *was* his real intent?

She had an opportunity to ask him that night, and, marvelling at her daring, anticipating a rebuff, she took the plunge.

'Are you really serious about that evacuation?'

He slitted his blue eyes at her. 'You mean Godmother and the girl?' he interpreted.

'Godmother Phyllida and Gillian,' Jessica said.

'You mean getting rid of them?'

'Yes.'

'Of course I am. Did you have any doubts?'

She said she had. 'Women ... I mean *some* women ... go for the he-man touch, and instead of discouraging Gillian today I think you might have aroused her.'

'Arouse?' he asked, aroused himself.

'Interested her, intrigued her. Even thrilled her.'

'Bloody hell!' he yelled. There was no doubt, Jessica accepted, of any real intent, not with that response.

Presently he asked in a more controlled voice: 'What is it you're getting at?'

'This,' Jessica answered. 'It's a well-known fact that the authoritarian approach often gets results.'

'Authoritarian?'

'The masterful man,' Jessica supplied, 'the dominating male. The upper hand type.'

'Well, you've experienced my control' ... control! Jessica squirmed ... 'did it arouse you?' While he waited for her reply he took out his smoke makings and began the rubbing and rolling process. To her secret dismay the dry whisper of the tobacco in his large tan palm, then the deliberate packing of the flattened weed, invoked her. When he licked the edges of the cigarette together, his tongue following the line of the rim, his narrowed blue eyes never leaving hers, she knew an odd excitation.

'I asked you a question, Miss Makin,' he said. As he always did, he was putting the completed cigarette into a case.

'No, Mr Fortescue,' she answered him, 'I was not aroused.'

Several moments went by in silence.

'So you suggest I try a soft approach?' Tim asked lazily. 'Get her thoroughly sick of me like kids get sick of chocolate cake?'

'If you're genuine about all this, yes,' Jessica replied.

'You should damn well know I'm genuine,' he burst out, 'I've told you often enough. What else do you want me to do? Take you to bed in front of Godmother and the girl so that the whole thing is spelled out once and for all?'

'No, I don't. I just suggested something different. Why not try it?' Aware of her burning cheeks, Jessica switched quickly to: 'How's my brother?' She had heard Tim earlier on the phone.

There was the slightest of hesitations, but it could not be because of Toby's health, for the report Tim gave Jessica was a harmless one.

'Same bulletin—doing as well as can be expected. Making fair progress, but slowly, leg still needing care—all the usual stuff. He seems as though he'll be at the Base for some time yet. I intend to fly over to see him.'

'Us, too?' It was Gillian, who had come into the room just in time to hear Tim's last words.

At the eagerness in her voice Tim glanced quickly at Jessica. He secretly raised one sardonic brow. It gave him a devil look, Jessica thought. The flick in his eyes conveyed clearly: 'Why bother with sugar as an offputter when there's such an anxiety for someone else?'

All the same, he said sweetly to the girl, 'Yes, I'll take you, my dear.'

Gillian looked a little stunned, but Godmother, close behind her, beamed.

Tim kept up the new approach for the rest of the week. He was extremely considerate and attentive to Gillian, and after her initial surprise Gillian was plainly pleased with herself. If nothing else she found his attention flattering. Godmother was obviously very happy—almost, Jessica thought, as though she saw a ring already on Gillian's hand.

But the experiment did not last long. Tim wearied of being fatuous, especially when the object of his over-attention did not seem to be wearying of him, as he had hoped. Secretly Jessica suspected that Gillian actually was only semi-aware of everything, all she really thought of was getting to the base and seeing Toby. But Jessica kept that suspicion to herself.

Then one morning Tim flew the two girls to the hospital. By car it would have taken hours, by air they were there in forty minutes—indeed it took longer to drive into the Flying Doctor Base than flying to the strip.

Toby was happy to see them. He kissed his sister and said the customary fond, insulting things, but he was very polite to Gillian. However, the formality did not fool Jessica. She found some pretence to go out of the room, leaving the two alone, as Tim had said he had business to do while he waited for them.

Tim was back again now, though, and sitting on the hospital verandah. He did not see Jessica at first, he was too self-absorbed. She looked at him covertly and thought he seemed worried, almost shut-in. Then he glanced up, saw her, and rose.

'Finished?' he asked.

'Gillian is still in there. I just came out for a moment.' She looked significantly at him; several times he had commented on a possible attraction between her brother and Gillian. But today there was no response.

'Are you concerned about something?' Jessica asked.

'No, of course not,' he snapped. 'How long before she's finished in there?' he added.

'Why, is it time to leave?' Jessica asked.

'It will be soon, and I wanted to have a word with your brother.'

'Go in now, then. Unless something has happened since I came out they won't be embarrassed.'

'A word *alone*,' he answered shortly.

Presently Gillian came out, eyes down, cheeks pink. Tim Fortescue went in, but he was not long.

'Come on, we'll push off,' he said the moment he returned. 'No landing lights where we're going.'

'Can we come again, Tim?' Gillian asked on the way to the strip where Tim's Cessna waited.

'I'll be coming,' Tim said in a flat voice. Gillian did not appear to hear the singular 'I', nor the flat tone, but Jessica did, and she wondered about it.

The following day Gillian suggested, seeing they were forbidden to swim in any waterhole, and seeing they had done the rest of the things, that they drive over to Falling Star.

'Falling Star?' Although she had come out from Sydney to see Toby's place of work Jessica was still surprised.

'It was actually your brother who suggested it,' Gillian submitted hopefully. 'It's not all that far, really; there and back would not be all that much further than a day's picnic. We could even tell Godmother we're having a picnic. Now that she's doing this cookbook thing she's not keeping tags on me all the time.'

'And what lie do you suggest for Tim? Or did you plan to tell him the truth, Gillian?' For some reason Jessica did not feel keen about the idea.

'Truth would be no advantage,' Gillian sighed. 'You know our Tim, he'd veto it at once—he's like that. And Jessica' . . . an appealing note in Gillian's voice . . . 'I want to go very much.'

'Well, I really don't know.' Jessica spoke truly; she didn't know; she even felt a cobweb of doubt about the suggestion.

'It's only two hundred kilometres away . . . two hours' driving.' Gillian murmured in a low voice. She added: '*Please*, Jessica!'

There was no reason to refuse, Jessica decided, the distance was fair enough, and even though they had never put the little car to that long a journey, and even though Tim had never thought they would, the car was actually quite road-worthy.

Nonetheless she still hesitated, and it was only after much persuasion that she agreed. She felt she should ask Harry, the S.D. mechanic, to look the car over, then O.K. it, but that might have drawn attention, alerted Harry to mention the request to the big boss, finally cancelled Gillian's much-desired journey.

Shrugging away that cobweb of doubt, Jessica agreed.

Godmother nodded affably when told that the girls would be out all day. She said that Timothy also would be away, and suggested to Alfred, who was quite cookbook-slanted these days, that they have an uninterrupted session in the kitchen.

The girls left moments after Tim left the next morning, but they departed by the southern track and then doubled back again in case they were noticed. It was sly, and Jessica felt guilty about it, but all the same she did it. She had a feeling they could be punished for their deceit; destiny had a mean habit of inflicting things like—well, in this case punctures, or dead engines, or something of the sort on wrongdoers.

'Yet actually we're doing nothing wrong,' Jessica said aloud.

Gillian did not answer; she was looking out on the same scenery as at S.D., but obviously seeing something else.

'No wonder he loves it,' she said, and Jesssica knew she was not referring to the owner of what she was looking at.

Jessica listened nervously for knocks in the engine all the way to Falling Star, but nothing occurred. They arrived at the satellite ... subsidiary ... Falling Star, call it whatever pleased you, several hours later, the little car performing perfectly.

'Why, it's a sweet place!' Gillian exclaimed delightedly.

'Home from home,' Jessica remembered from Toby's enthusiastic letters to her. 'Now where's this old Tim Browning?'

'I don't know.' Gillian's voice had changed from delight to doubt, and, taking her eyes off the track long enough to follow the direction of Gillian's fearful glance, Jessica saw why.

For there *was* a Tim on the verandah of Falling Star, but it was not an old Tim. This younger Tim was a very familiar Tim, and as he watched them drive up he wore an enigmatical expression.

'It's Tim Fortescue, not Tim Browning!' Gillian exclaimed. 'I didn't know he was coming over here, did you?'

'No,' Jessica agreed grimly, 'I did not.'

To herself, recognising that shut-in look that Tim had worn on the day he had sat on the verandah of the Base Hospital, Jessica added: 'Something is wrong.'

She stopped the engine and they got out.

'Surprise! Surprise!' Tim drawled sarcastically.

'It wasn't meant to be.' Jessica decided on honesty. 'We wouldn't have told you if you hadn't found out.'

He shrugged carelessly as though the matter

was of little importance to him, and feeling rather small the two girls followed him into the home-stead.

'So this is where Toby lives,' Gillian, recovered, said in a low voice.

'I'll ask old Tim which is his room if you like, and you can attach a plaque "Toby sleeps here".' Sarcasm came readily to Tim's lips.

Jessica darted him an angry look, but he was bringing Tim Browning in to meet them. Tim was quite aged now, Jessica noted, he must be well on the way to retirement. She wondered if Toby had any ambitions to take over. He would love such a job. Then she saw Johann, their S.D. bookkeeper, behind old Tim. So he, too, had come across. As the gallant Johann kissed both the ladies' hands, again Jessica was aware of that cobweb of doubt. Why, she wondered, had Tim brought his accountant here?

Old Tim was frankly enjoying the company. He was missing Toby around the place, he said. With Gillian's help he made a huge pot of tea, and they sat and drank it. The conversation did not lag, but Jessica found she could not join in. Gillian on the other hand was quite animated, obviously enjoying herself, but Jessica had never felt so inexplicably low in all her life as she felt now.

Something is wrong, she thought again.

On Tim's advice . . . Tim Fortescue, not Tim Browning . . . they left before the official party. Jessica named it that. By going first, Tim said, if they had a breakdown help would not be far behind.

But nothing went wrong, and they arrived back at S.D. in good time, Godmother still in the kitchen taking notes, Gillian soon filling the house with a happy little song, then, not long after, Tim Fortescue walking in.

'Enjoy your trip?' he asked Jessica, taking off his wide hat and tossing it accurately across to the table.

'Yes.' Something urged Jessica to ask: 'Did you?'

'No,' he said. He stood at the opposite end of the room to where she stood and looked levelly at her. 'No, I did not.'

A minute went past, and a minute in absolute silence can be a long time.

'I'm going into the Base Hospital tomorrow,' he announced. A pause. 'I'll be going alone.'

'But——' Jessica started.

'*Alone.* You can tell her that.'

'Her?' she queried.

'Gillian. You can also tell yourself.'

'I've just been told,' said Jessica.

'Then you understand?'

'I understand,' she assured coldly. 'You don't want us.'

'Require you is my word.'

'Nor want,' she persisted.

He ignored that. 'I just wanted to inform you,' he said stonily. Without another word he went out.

Jessica went out, too, and what she had to tell to Gillian stopped the little tune Gillian had been humming.

'Tim is going to the hospital tomorrow,' Gillian echoed, 'and not taking us!'

'Some business thing, I expect,' Jessica shrugged. 'Anyway, we're not wanted . . . I mean required.'

'But why? *Why?*'

'I don't know, Gillian, but I do know that if you don't want the shower, I do. I love this Centre, but it does turn you a rusty-red.'

Jessica went into the bathroom, undressed and turned on the hot tap. She wished she could be like the girl in the song and wash Tim Fortescue and all the annoyances he continually caused her out of her hair.

Vaguely, only half consciously, as in a dream, Jessica awoke in the night . . . or was it the early morning? She could not have said what aroused her, and certainly there was no noise. She lay very still listening, remembering her first night here at S.D. and Tim Fortescue's impudent knock on the window. Was Tim wandering around now? His mood had been a very odd one of late.

She listened intently, then decided she must have imagined it all. She drifted off again.

She evidently was not the only one who had had a disturbed night, for Gillian did not appear at the breakfast table, and as her bedroom door was firmly closed, indicating that she did not want to be wakened, Jessica left her alone.

She did not see her during the morning.

Just before lunch, or the time they usually took

lunch, the telephone in the hallway pealed, and as there was no one else around Jessica answered it.

'Jessie' . . . it was Tim Fortescue . . . 'I want you over here immediately.'

So he still had not left S.D. for the hospital! Jessica mulled that over for a moment, then mumbled: 'It's near mealtime. Can't it wait?'

'You heard me. Immediately! Now come across.' His phone slammed down.

Confused, half angry, half curious, muttering insulting things about him under her breath, Jessica crossed the yellow grass to his office. She went in, deliberately not knocking as it said on the door.

Tim was standing waiting for her, arms folded, face grim. He nodded to the desk. There were several written reports there.

'Read them,' he ordered. 'Read them right through, then read them through again. Make sure you understand what's in them before I tell you the only way out.' A pause, then: 'Your way out.' Now a longer pause. '. . . *His*.'

'His?' Jessica barely breathed it.

'Your brother's.'

'Toby's?'

'Yes.'

'Toby? But where does Toby come in? What has Toby done?'

Tim Fortescue only repeated: 'Read these papers.'

He stood waiting while she did.

CHAPTER SEVEN

JESSICA had accepted the sheets, and now she began to scan them. After half a page she stared incredulously up at Tim, then, at a prompting nod from him, she lowered her gaze again and read on.

She reached the end of the page and took up a second. There was not much on the third and last page, but she read to the end.

It was a long time before she could bring herself to look at Tim a second time, but when she did he was waiting for her.

'Go through it all again,' he demanded.

'I don't want to. It's all lies,' Jessica protested.

'All the same, go through it,' he ordered.

Jessica took up the papers and repeated the torture. For torture it was, she thought. It wasn't true, it could never have happened, but reading it, and knowing someone believed it had happened, seared her.

At last she put the pages down—finally down.

'Toby would never do this,' she said quietly.

'Nonetheless it has been done,' Tim replied.

'Someone else——'

'There's no one else who could do it, except old Tim, and I'd stake my life on old Tim Browning.'

'But not on young Toby Makin?' she said with

a break in her voice.

'Well, I don't know him, do I?'

'You know me.'

'Do I?' he said again, and reached in his pocket for the makings of the cigarette he never smoked.

But when the whispering of the weed, the rubbing, the flattening, the packing and the licking together process was over, this time he did put the cigarette in his mouth. He ignited a match, and it made a little scratchy noise like a small marauding mouse, Jessica thought blankly. Her mind seemed a blank. She saw Tim Fortescue narrowing his eyes at her through a blue weave of smoke.

'Falling Star is' ... he gave an amount that made Jessica wince ... '—— dollars short.'

'It can't be!' Thank heaven the blankness was leaving her, that she could fight back.

'You've seen the balances yourself. Figures can't lie.'

'All right then, but it couldn't be Toby.'

'It couldn't be Tim. I've known old Tim all my life, my father knew him. I would——'

'You would stake your life on Tim,' Jessica said before he could.

A silence came between them. Only when a clock chimed somewhere outside did they begin to speak again.

'Why would Toby do it?' Jessica asked. 'He had a job he loved, he was contented—why, I think he would even have worked here for nothing.'

'Not for ——' Again, cruelly, Tim stated the

sum that was missing.

'Toby has never been the money sort,' Jessica defended hotly. 'He never seemed to need money.'

'Not for himself, perhaps, but—for someone else?'

Jessica bridled at that.

'I've never been money-minded, either,' she retorted, 'even though I've been out of work Toby never felt an obligation to look after me.'

'You're on the wrong track,' Tim said levelly. 'What about—Gillian?'

'Gillian?' she gasped.

'He fell in love with Gillian. I saw it the first time he met her—even blind Freddy would have seen it.' A pause. 'The discrepancies started then.'

'But why? *Why?*' Jessica cried more than said it.

'Because your brother was at a distinct disadvantage compared to me,' Tim said matter-of-factly, and Jessica stiffened. She supposed that actually Toby was, but did this impossible man have to cry out his superiority quite so loudly?

'Your brother could see,' Tim went on, 'that my godmother had Gillian all set up for me, set up for the big boss. Holy cow, who couldn't see it? What hope had a mere bookkeeper against that? But money could help, your brother would think. At least it would get him away, put him on a better footing for the girl of his choice.'

'If that was the case would Toby be where he is now?' Jessica demanded. 'Being at the Base isn't getting away.'

'The hospital incident would be unplanned,'
Tim shrugged. He waited a moment, then he said
significantly: 'Also how do we know he's there
now?'

'At the Flying Doctor Base? Of course he's
there. Why, you're—— I mean you were going to
visit him.'

'True. But after digesting this' . . . Tim leaned
over and tapped the reports . . . 'I've decided first
to see if the bird has flown.'

'Flown? Toby? You're mad!' she exclaimed.
'He would never do that.'

'Nonetheless would you like to get on the
phone and ring on your own account?' Not waiting for her answer, he took up the telephone and
handed it to Jessica.

'I have to go through the homestead first, don't
I?' Jessica asked.

'You know you do,' he said.

'But Gillian is asleep. She must have been very
tired last night, she never came in for breakfast.'
Jessica stopped short, her mind running in too
many channels at the one time. Gillian couldn't
have—— Oh, no, now she was being mad.

'Oh, didn't she?' Tim took the phone back
from Jessica and dialled the number himself.

After a long time it was answered by Alf.
Evidently the cook had had to come from the
kitchen.

'Is the young lady around, Alf?' Tim asked
briskly.

'Her door is still closed, boss. The missus' . . .

Alf always spoke of Godmother as missus ...
'said to let her rest. We're doing Drover's
Dream, boss: mutton chops, onions, turnips ...
Yes, boss. Yes.' Jessica could hear Alf's suddenly
respectful attention to Tim instead of Drover's
Dream. 'Yes, I'll get you the base at once.'

In minutes Tim was through.

Now Tim spoke quietly, and Jessica could not
hear the response. She sat on the edge of the
chair folding and unfolding her hands, trying to
think, trying not to think, trying to go blank,
trying for action.

She heard the phone go down.

'He's gone,' said Tim.

'Gone? Toby has left the hospital? He couldn't
have!'

'Yet he has. He signed himself out before
breakfast. He was fairly recovered, the Matron
just told me, but they would have preferred to
keep him longer for observation. However, if a
patient insists on discharging himself ...' Tim
shrugged.

Jessica said bleakly: 'Where could he have
gone?'

'With an amount like that one on the report he
could go a damn long way,' Tim answered
shortly.

'He wouldn't!' Jessica insisted with spirit.

'Then more fool him—the arm of the law may
be long, but the further you get away the better
chance you have.'

'You're hateful!' Jessica said now.

'Well, wouldn't you be in my position?'

'The way I see your position is this,' Jessica answered. 'You've suffered an unfortunate loss, and I won't deny that, but you can't say, not really, what's the true source of the loss.'

'No? Why do you think I took Johann across there yesterday? To see the scenery?'

Jessica had no answer to that.

'I'll put it as clearly as I can,' Tim said presently. 'That amount of money' . . . he nodded to the report . . . 'is definitely missing. It's cash. Stockmen don't like cheques, they insist on the real folding and jingling stuff. Because they're out most of the time they only collect their pay monthly, sometimes longer than that. Naturally it grows.'

'And is kept where?' broke in Jessica.

'A drawer in the office. It doesn't sound the most secure place, but only two people use the office, only two people use the house—Browning, Makin. The men's quarters are at least a kilometre away, and the pay, when they ask for it, is taken out to them, they don't come in. There's never been any trouble, not a breath of it, until——'

'Until Makin signed on.' Jessica's voice was thin.

'You said it,' Tim told her.

Another minute went by.

'What are you going to do?' Jessica broke the quiet in desperation.

He took his time in answering. He brought out his makings again, but changed his mind and put them back in his pocket.

Then he said deliberately: 'That all depends on you.'

She looked at him in surprise; he knew she had been out of work when she came here.

'I'm sorry,' she stammered, 'I haven't anything like that amount, and there's nowhere I could go to try to raise it. You see, the parents, Toby's and my parents, died some years ago, and——' She stopped at a negative shake of his head.

'That was not what I meant,' he said.

'Then?'

Now his look was inscrutable; she could not have guessed what he was thinking until he told her.

'There are other ways of cancelling a debt,' he said.

'Like?'

'Before I put it in one word . . . yes, it can be put in one word . . . I'll admit to you that bringing you into S.D. hasn't been a success. The women are still here; I don't want them here; I won't have them. I want the Fortescue house as my father had it, as his father had it before him— a man's place.'

'Yet not all the time,' Jessica broke in. 'Your father existed. You exist. That, quite clearly, had to be brought about by two. A man—*and a woman*.' She looked triumphantly at him.

He looked equally triumphantly back at Jessica.

'Hasn't it occurred to you that we might not have been conceived here?' he asked.

'I don't know about your father,' Jessica retorted, 'but I think I know about you. You were never conceived anywhere. You're not flesh and blood. You're—you're iron!'

'A change, anyway,' he said sarcastically, 'from beef.' He waited a moment. 'Look, Jessie,' he said more reasonably, 'all this is getting us nowhere, getting you nowhere with Toby, me nowhere with two women whom I don't want and won't have. Oh, yes, I know you think I should show them the door if I'm really serious, but how can I do that to old Godmother, to the only woman I ever knew who really touched my heart . . . that is, until——' But he did not finish.

She waited, and presently he went on.

'But there is a way out, a way that will send Godmother packing promptly, admitting defeat, kissing me a fond farewell.' A long, deliberate pause this time. Then: 'Also—kissing you.'

'Kissing—kissing me? Why? What on earth do you mean?' Jessica stared at him, completely confused.

'Kissing the bride and groom. Kissing Mr and Mrs Fortescue. You see, you would be Mrs Fortescue. How could Godmother have plans for Gillian after that?'

'I . . . marry . . . you . . .' she stammered.

'Yes,' he said.

'But I would never do it,' Jessica gasped.

'Not for your own sake, but—your brother's? You see, the moment we went through the ceremony I would tear up the evidence of my loss. But if not . . .' He shrugged.

'There must be other ways,' Jessica said desperately.

'Think of just one,' he came back.

'You'd be a fool,' she pointed out, 'you'd be defeating your own purpose. You don't want a wife, yet you would be taking a wife.' She looked challengingly at him.

'But a wife I could discard,' he said. 'Such things are done easily these days. Gillian I couldn't have discarded, not with Godmother around.' He gave a low laugh.

'They'd know why you were doing it,' Jessica said. 'How could you stand in front of a preacher while they watched, *knowing*?'

'But they wouldn't be watching,' he replied.

'Godmother not watch her godson being married?' Jessica scorned.

'No,' he answered.

'Then what would you say to them when we went away to—to do it?' Jessica blurted uncomfortably.

'Nothing, because we wouldn't go away. It would be done, as you put it, here.'

'In that case they would have to see,' Jessica persisted. 'You couldn't lock them out.'

'I said *here*,' he persisted in his turn, 'in this office. No need even to leave the room. Now that really is a convenient marriage, don't you agree?'

'You're crazy!' she said angrily.

'I'm in full possession of my not inconsiderable senses,' he retorted. 'I am also, at the moment, in possession of a dog-collar man.'

'What?'

'Minister—preacher—reverend, call him what

you wish. We call our outback padre simply Bill. Pastor Bill Flett is actually the name. Bill has a huge diocese. Some of his flock he doesn't see for years. Often when he can't get around, and love and nature decide that things can't wait, he performs a marriage and a baptism at the same time. But' . . . a keen look at Jessica . . . 'that won't happen to us.'

'Thank you,' she said drily.

'Oh, no, thank the fact that I don't want you any more than you want me, Jessie, that your privacy will never be encroached on, that the only difference to you would be your name, and you could drop that if you liked. Oh' . . . a reminding nod . . . 'and the welcome difference of peace of mind concerning your brother.'

'This isn't happening,' Jessica muttered in unbelief.

'It is happening,' he told her, 'so face up to it. Face up to the fact, too, that in the next office the Reverend Bill is giving a marriage guidance talk to one of my misguided stockmen, who has a hunch he would like to return to married bliss, poor fool.'

'It's incredible!' Jessica was still unbelieving.

'The Reverend Bill is a busy man,' Tim went on, 'he has to leave within the hour.' He actually yawned the information more than stated it.

'But marriages can't be performed that quickly,' Jessica protested. It was slowly sinking into her that this man really meant what he was saying.

'Don't tell me you want the bridesmaid, page-boy bit? The wedding cake? The bells?' Tim taunted.

'I said marriage, not the accoutrements of marriage,' Jessica answered. 'There have to be forms and things.' She added: 'Pre-arrangements.'

'There was a pre-arrangement.'

'For Gillian?'

'Don't be daft!' he snapped.

'Then it couldn't have been for——'

'Strange though it may seem it was, and is, for you. Right from the first day you came here I knew I could pull it off with you—that escape, I mean. I got in touch with our padre and told him I was contemplating marriage. No hurry, I wrote, just get the preliminaries done, the ring ready, then meander over at your leisure.'

'You really meant no likelihood of a baptism and a wedding together,' Jessica said a little hysterically. She felt at the end of her tether.

'Precisely,' he grinned. 'But Bill came at the right time. The right time for me, but particularly the right time for you . . . regarding your brother. The moment you say Yes, put your signature on a certificate, your brother is free.'

'And I'm tied?' she cried.

'Look,' he said coolly, 'there are eight bedrooms over there in the homestead, and after we take up occupancy as Mr and Mrs Fortescue there'll be six left over.' He paused. 'Not seven, as you seem to think.'

'Oh, no, I don't think,' Jessica corrected. She bit her lip. 'How long will the farce go on?'

'Please yourself,' he shrugged. 'You might even

care to enjoy a little time as Mrs Boss.'

'I doubt it,' she shrugged back. Her next question was: 'What would be expected of me?'

'Absolutely nothing. Not even a goodnight kiss, which, incidentally, you seemed to have been short of during our so-named dalliance. I very much wanted Godmother to see, but you cheated me there.'

'Are you' . . . Jessica stammered . . . 'thinking of cheating me now?'

'What do you mean?' he demanded.

'Will those six rooms left unoccupied be—seven, after all?' she asked.

'Perish the thought!' he came back at once. 'Well, not unless you requested it, unless you wanted it.'

'Perish the thought,' Jessica echoed.

There was a silence for a few moments. Jessica resumed first.

'And your wants?' she probed.

'Like the rest of me, under control,' he assured her. 'Though——'

'Though?' she asked quickly.

'Though if I did "want", as you schoolgirlishly put it, you would be wasting your time locking a door. But' . . . before she could break in . . . 'I won't be "wanting".'

He folded his arms and stood before her.

'Well, Jessie Makin?'

'It would have to be Jessica Makin on a certificate,' Jessica mumbled.

'Meaning?' he demanded.

'What else is there for me to do?' she replied.

'Exactly.' He crossed the room and opened a door. 'Ready when you are, Reverend Bill.' He turned round to Jessica. 'Did you want a bouquet? These will do.' He took some Salvation Jane out of a bottle on his desk.

'The big boss has flowers!' Jessica was surprised.

'Not bloody likely, not these kind, anyway. They're here to be sent down to the Pastoral Board for suggestions for eradication. They're becoming too much of a pest.—Ah, Bill!'

The Reverend Bill Flett had walked in, taken Jessica's hand and smiled encouragingly at her. For the first time since she had come into this room half an hour ... and a thousand years ... ago, Jessica knew a measure of peace.

She stood with the blue Salvation Jane in her hand ... had anyone anywhere ever been married holding a bunch of noxious weed?

She heard Tim's dog-collar man say: 'Dearly beloved, we are gathered together here in the sight of God, and in the face of this congregation' ... looking round she saw several of the stockies, ten-gallon hats in their hands, at the door ... 'to join together this man and this woman in Holy Matrimony ...'

She heard from Tim: 'I, Timothy Fortescue ...'

She intoned: 'I, Jessica Makin ...'

Then it was all over. Someone kissed her. Was it the Reverend Bill? Or one of the cattlemen? Or was it——

'Come on,' said Tim, 'we'll go over to the

homestead together, hear the bombshell burst.'
He went ahead.

As they reached the door, the telephone pealed,
and he went back to answer it.

Clearly Jessica could hear Alf's: 'It's Falling
Star ringing you, boss. And something else, boss,
and you'll never believe it.'

'Later, Alf,' said Tim. 'Put on old Tim.'

The rest Jessica could not hear, but she could
see Tim's face. At least she could see his face in
the beginning of the conversation, then deliberately he turned away from her, cupping the
phone so only he could listen.

'Go on,' she heard him say in a low voice. 'Yes.
Yes.'

Eventually he put the phone down and joined
her. In absolute silence they crossed the yellow
turf to the large square house—the house, Jessica
thought a little wildly, of eight bedrooms, six left
over after two of them were occupied. Not seven.

The silence suddenly wanted to make her
laugh. What a strange bridal procession, she
thought.

At her first giggle, he stopped her sternly.

'Cool it, Jessie—because you'll need to be cool.
There's something that has to be said.'

'Yes?' she asked.

'That ring was from Tim Browning.'

'Yes, I heard his voice.'

'But not what he said, I think.'

'No,' Jessica agreed, 'I didn't hear.'

Without any preamble, any preparation, any
hint of what was to come, Tim said: 'It was all a

mistake—the missing money, I mean. Tim had forgotten that he hadn't put the money in the drawer after all. He was terribly sorry. He said it was about time stumps were drawn for him, that he was too old for the job, and' . . . grimly . . . 'he is. He said it was lucky that no harm was done.'

'No harm!' Jessica had stopped in her tracks. She only started walking again when Tim's arm impelled her.

'For the love of heaven,' he appealed, 'at least let us get inside. Look at those fools!' He nodded to the stockmen shadow-clapping them.

Alf was at the open door, and he was fairly bursting with excitement.

'She's gone,' he said, 'the missus has left. She was writing down the ingredients for Drover's Dream when the young one rang. It seems the young one wasn't in her bedroom at all, it seems that she took off in the car in the very early hours' . . . Jessica remembered *her* early hours, remembered faintly hearing something, then slipping off again . . . 'it seems she went and married young Toby Makin, then rang here and broke the news to the missus. The missus was quite bucked, she told me she liked Toby right from the first, that she thought after all it might be the best. The Cessna came in with the mail, and the missus was on it like a shot. Sent you her love, boss. Said she'd be in touch. Things happen, don't they?'

'Don't they?' said Tim. He looked at Jessica.

Slowly, painfully, laboriously, Jessica enunciated: 'So we needn't have——'

'No,' Tim answered, 'we needn't have.'

Presently he said: 'Under those circumstances I don't think I need carry the bride into the house.'

CHAPTER EIGHT

IT was ten hours later, and Jessica was lying on a different bed in a different room . . . but a room in the same house.

Tim Fortescue had insisted on the move.

'As missus, which you are now, Jessie, you have to have the master bedroom.' He had paused. 'But without the master,' he had re-assured her.

'My old room suited me perfectly,' Jessica had tried to decline.

'But it wouldn't suit Alf. Alf is a stickler for doing things properly. He would expect missus to have the best.'

'I'm not married to Alf,' she pointed out.

'No, but you are married to his boss, and as such . . .' Tim had shrugged.

'Where do *you* sleep?' Jessica had asked suspiciously.

'Have no fears,' he had allayed, 'I'm even further now from you than I was before.'

'Not that it made any difference,' Jessica had reminded him, 'when you could communicate through a window.'

'All that's over,' he had said magnanimously. 'Now that we're man and wife we can communicate legitimately by the hall.' She had looked at him alarmed, and he had explained at once: 'In, of course, a case of emergency. Now shut up, Miss Makin . . . I mean Mrs Fortescue . . . and help me carry your things to the new room.'

The new room was large, airy, in every way superior. Also unarguably intended for two. With one only occupying it, it seemed distinctly empty.

Now Jessica lay in the big four-poster to which the first Fortescue had brought his bride, she supposed. The marriage had lasted briefly, the same as their son's marriage, the same as the son's son's . . . and hers . . . would be brief.

A marriage of convenience, she mused, that had turned out an inconvenience, that need not have happened at all.

She closed her eyes, opened them, watched the curtains at the window hanging still and straight in the warm, windless air. She refused to believe the things that had happened today. She could not, *she simply could not*, be Mrs Tim Fortescue. Yet, feeling the third finger on her left hand, she wore a ring.

'Was this ring your mother's?' she had asked Tim, looking at the plain gold band and twisting it around.

'Hell, no,' he had said, 'I wouldn't want a ring of hers. No, the Reverend Bill brought it. He carries wedding rings as a kind of stock-in-trade. Otherwise you would have had to use a curtain ring, and there's very few curtains at S.D.'

'Do I get an engagement ring?' Jessica had asked flippantly.

'You were never engaged,' he reminded her. 'I wanted you to be, but it never got to that.'

'It got much further,' Jessica had sighed.

'If that sigh is for an engagement ring I'll give you one that will make everyone sigh,' he had told her. 'S.D. is very close to the opal country. I'll fly you over to the diggings one day, let you choose a ring for yourself.'

'I won't be here,' she had reminded him.

'Leaving me that soon, are you? I thought that at least you'd wait until your brother got back.'

'Back where?' Jessica had enquired.

'Falling Star, of course. He'll be the boss. Old Tim is very happy to step down—in fact he insisted on it. He wants to visit his daughter in Sydney, then when he comes back he wants to move to a shack near the stockmen. He doesn't fancy being the third in a house.'

'Third?' Jessica had been puzzled.

'Well, where did you think Gillian would live?' Tim had demanded.

'In the city, the same as your grandmother did, and your mother.' Jessica had paused, then added: 'The same as I will.'

'That happens to the Fortescues, not to other people,' he had stated. 'Young Gillian quite likes it up here. Also she's in love. She and your brother should make a good cattle couple.'

'Which is very important, isn't it? A good cattle couple,' Jessica had retorted contemptuously. Because of the warning look on his face she had gone on hastily: 'What about Godmother Phyllida? What will she do with no chicks to scheme for?'

'Are you serious?' he had grinned. 'That old

pest will be busier than ever, visiting both here and Falling Star to check up on her great-god-children.' For all his apparent unkindness Tim's voice had been affectionate.

'There'll only be Falling Star's to check,' Jessica had reminded him.

'Of course.'

As was only to be expected in a close community like S.D., it had taken Alf no more than several minutes to learn what had happened over at Administration. The stockmen who had been called upon to witness the ceremony had seen to that.

'If I'd known I would have made a wedding cake,' Alf had said. 'I can, you know, miss . . . no, missus now, isn't it? . . . it's not only cut and come again cake and brownie with Alf. But anyway' . . . proudly . . . 'there'll be the Drover's Dream for your wedding dinner. I put my best into it to show the old missus how outback tucker can be better than all that French stuff.'

'Thank you, Alf,' the young missus had murmured faintly.

'What on earth *is* Drover's Dream?' Jessica had asked Tim when Alf had gone busily out. 'I heard Alf say over the phone that it was mutton chops, onions and turnips, but what is it?'

'It's mutton chops, onions and turnips,' Tim said. 'Most suitable, wouldn't you say?'

'Most,' Jessica had agreed. 'I even think I'll change out of my jeans, arrange my Salvation Jane in the middle of the table. At times like these we should let our heads go.'

'Now don't get too reckless,' Tim had advised. '*I* possess the strength to break down *your* bedroom door, but I doubt if *you* have the strength to break down *mine*.'

'I don't care for that kind of conversation,' Jessica had frowned.

'You started it,' he had come back. 'However, you'll be pleasantly surprised with Drover's Dream, especially when it's washed down with champagne.'

'Champagne?'

'What did you expect? Beer?'

'I really don't know. I've never married a cattleman before.'

'Have you married anyone before?' he had asked with interest.

'No. Have you?'

'Perish the thought . . . also, if you can, put on a bridal expression. Here comes the Drover's Dream.'

Instead of bringing in piled plates as he always did, Alf had acknowledged the occasion by ladling their dinner into a large solid silver dish.

'All right, boss?' he asked of the dish.

'Excellent, Alf. And what is this?'

'Candles,' said Alf triumphantly, and he placed their several emergency candles held in case the electric plant failed on the table. They were balanced in empty jam jars, still wearing their labels, but Alf lit the candles proudly.

'Dinner by candlelight,' he said.

A gurgle of laughter had risen in Jessica, but she had conquered it.

When Alf went out, though, the gurgle escaped, and Tim's laughter joined hers.

It was a good beginning for a meal that proved surprisingly good, that certainly deserved the Fortescue silver plate on which it was presented.

'Tonight the Drover's Dream is even better than my dreams when I was a drover,' Tim said. 'I wonder why that is.'

'Candlelight,' Jessica suggested. She mused: 'So you were once a drover?'

'My father believed in me doing everything,' Tim replied. 'Dipping, drafting, horn-trimming, branding, the lot. I can even sing the cattle if needs be. You do that at night when you're over-landing and cop a cranky beast. Want to hear me?'

'Yes.'

'A romantic song or a Western?'

'Western,' Jessica said firmly.

He sang it robustly, undoubtedly helped by the champagne that was going down very fast.

'As well as improving the Drover's Dream I think candlelight has improved your voice,' Jessica commended.

Tim rose and turned off their electric power so that only the emergency candles lit the table. Then unexpectedly, evidently following another train of thought, he blew out the candles.

'You're lovely, Jessie,' he said.

'When it's dark?' she baited him.

'All the time, missus, I've noticed it before. But I have to say you look even lovelier in the dark of night.'

'Then take a good look,' she tossed flippantly, standing up for him to do so, 'because you'll never be seeing me again without light.'

'No?' he asked quietly.

'No,' she said.

Alf came in with tinned plum pudding which neither of them wanted, but accepted politely, clicked his tongue at the extinguished candles and lit them again.

They ploughed through the canned duff, left Alf to clear away, then went to the lounge. Here Tim played his music, classical this time since romance was needed no longer, and, replete with food, soothed by Debussy, slightly drifting from champagne, presently Jessica slipped off.

She awoke, but not entirely, when Tim lifted her up in his arms.

'You've had a long day, missus,' he said softly, 'I'm putting you to bed.'

'No!' Jessica protested, trying to come out of her drowsiness but finding it hard.

He ignored her completely and carried her to her room. This room.

'Where's your nightie?' he asked.

'There. I mean—— No—no, leave it to me. Tim—Tim—you promised, Tim——'

'I said I'd be in the room down the hall,' he answered serenely, 'and so I will. But you're dead on your feet, little possum, so I'm going to put you to bed first.'

Before she could do anything about it, he had undone buttons, pulled zippers, tugged upward, pulled downward.

It was all over in minutes. In minutes again he left, closing the door behind him.

But the sleepy girl he had put to bed had sat up, wide awake.

Awake . . . and aroused.

Eventually Jessica did sleep. When she opened her eyes and looked at her watch she saw that her late oblivion had made for a late morning. She wondered what Alf would say when she went along for breakfast at nine-thirty.

But there was no Alf. Feeling relieved, Jessica made coffee and toast. She wondered if by chance Tim, too, had overslept, and if so, should she take him something. She went down the hall until she reached his room. Then, not sure what to do, she put her ear to the door.

'Trying to break it down already?' His voice came booming at her from the end of the passage. 'I felt I was irresistible, but not irresistible that quickly.'

'I thought you were in bed,' Jessica stammered.

'Obviously.'

'Oh, you fool!' she snapped, and turned back. 'Alf wasn't in the kitchen so I made my own breakfast and came along to ask you if you, too, would like something.'

'I breakfasted hours ago,' he told her.

'Alf cooked it for you?'

'I cooked my own. Alf is sensitive. He doesn't like being around too early with newlyweds.'

'Early at ten o'clock!' she exclaimed.

'I was up five hours ago, missus.'

'Well, I'll never be up by five.'

'Please yourself,' he shrugged, 'but don't expect Alf. He feels that mornings are private affairs. Though evidently not at this hour, because here he comes now.'

Tim turned and left.

Alf went through the breakfast explanation in his turn, his eyes discreetly down as he did so.

'I'll do my collecting from the store in the morning,' he told Jessica, 'and by the time I get over here you'll both be up, dressed and getting around. Now' ... embarrassed ... 'I thought steak for today, missus. It's beef country, so you can't have mutton too often.'

'Thank you, Alf,' Jessica said meekly, 'we're in your hands.'

Alf was flattered. 'I can see this is going to be a good thing,' he said.

'What, Alf?' Jessica asked.

'This wedding of yours and the boss's. About time the Fortescues had a fair go. Those other missuses were no good. I remember the last Mrs F. very well, and I was a lad here when the one before her began it all—the clearing out, I mean. But I can tell you're different.'

'Thank you,' said Jessica.

But when Tim came in for lunch he had no praise for the new régime.

'I would have been better off if I'd kept my finger out of the matrimonial pie,' he grumbled. 'You've certainly started something, Miss Makin.'

'Mrs Fortescue,' she corrected. 'What did I

start?'

He gave her a long look at the correction, but went on with his complaint.

'Two of the stockmen are asking about the housing situation,' he said. 'They never told me why, but it sticks out a mile. They're wanting their wives here.'

'Well?'

'It's not well,' he snapped. 'This is a man's place.'

'An all-the-way man?' Jessica enquired blandly, recalling the tag.

'Who told you that?' he demanded.

'Gillian. She said that the men out here used to be called the all-the-way men.'

'Not just called, they were. They are. We pride ourselves on our maleness, on our——'

'On your beef that builds tough boys,' Jessica nodded. 'Well, it's beef for dinner tonight. You only have Drover's Dream for special occasions like weddings, because this is the beef machine.'

'And no dreams permitted,' he nodded. 'I understand.'

After lunch, Jessica found a magazine and took it out to the shadiest of the verandahs. She sank down in the banana chair that Godmother always had claimed. What am I doing here? she thought. I'm a fraud. We both are frauds. But he, Tim, is at least paying for it all, I'm just a freeloader. What *am* I doing here? How long can I stay?

'Missus,' called Alf from inside, 'phone!'

Jessica went in again and took up the receiver. It was Toby and Gillian, both talking happily together. Jessica tolerated it until she could stand the babble no longer.

'One at a time!' she stipulated. 'You, Gillian.' She added encouragingly: 'Sister.'

'You don't mind?' Gillian asked anxiously.

'I'm happy, Gillian. Only you might have told me.'

'Then you might have told Aunt Phyllida, and she could have been difficult.'

'She wasn't, though, was she?'

'No, I think she's as delighted with Toby as I am.' Gillian sounded almost deliriously happy.

'Toby directed me to go out to Falling Star,' Gillian related. 'Remember, Jessica, I told you that.'

'Yes,' said Jessica, 'you told me.'

'It was to "case" the place, he said . . . see if I could live there.' A pause. 'I could live in a ditch with Toby.'

'I don't think you ever will, Gillian. Tim is very ambitious for Toby,' Jessica assured her.

'Rightly so—Toby can do anything,' Gillian claimed proudly. 'And you, sister Jessica, you *really* haven't minded?'

'Of course not,' Jessica repeated. She wondered why there were no congratulations from their end of the wire, didn't they know the *other* news?

Toby came on, and Jessica knew at once that neither of them had been told.

'We did the deed at Alice Springs, Sis,' he recounted. 'We're staying another few days, then making for home again.'

'Home?' asked Jessica, pretending she was uninformed.

'The Star. Have to settle down some time.' A pause. 'What about you?'

'Well—I'll wait until you get back,' Jessica said cautiously, 'then I'll see.'

'Then we'll both see,' Toby agreed. ''Bye, Sis.' His end went down.

Jessica stood by the old-fashioned receiver. Again she thought, What am I doing here? How long can I stay?

I can't stay any longer, she decided at last. Gillian is gone, Godmother has gone, so why am I here? The only thing for me to do is ask Tim for enough money to see me back to Sydney ... he promised me that ... and pack my bags.

She never thought of what would happen after that, she found she could only think so far. But she did go in and pack her bag and rehearse her speech for Tim.

At six o'clock Alf found her and said that dinner was cooked.

'What about the boss?' she asked. Now why had she said that?

'The boss always eats with the boys on Thursdays,' Alf informed her.—Was it Thursday? Jessica wondered.

The cook led her to the dining room, everything the same as last night, except for one setting only ... and no candles.

No candles.

Jessica sat in the darkling room, not bothering to get up and switch on the plant. She wondered why Alf's potatoes were so salty, for he really was a *very* good cook. Then she realised she was crying.

Alf came in to see if Missus wanted anything else. He switched on the light, saying that the days were getting shorter, and while he did Jessica brushed away the tears.

'I'll take the dishes away, wash them and then sign off,' he told Jessica.

'Don't you sleep here, Alf?' she asked. The homestead, she thought, was large enough for a retinue of helpers. Eight bedrooms, six not occupied.

'Oh, no, missus, and it's not because of you and the boss, I've always slept across at the barracks. The only thing different now is——'

'Breakfast,' Jessica nodded. 'Thank you, Alf.'

Alf nodded and went out. She could hear him in the kitchen clattering dishes. Presently she heard a door shut and knew that he had finished for the day.

She went into the lounge and examined Tim's records, selected several, played them, then realised she was not listening.

The telephone rang. She went into the hall to answer it, but, her hand on the receiver, she stopped. It would not be for her; only her brother knew she was here and he already had rung. It would not be from Tim, it would be for Tim, so let him deal with it. She looked at the guide on the wall, then put the call through to the canteen. Alf had said that the boss would be eating with the boys.

She decided to go to bed.

She had been in bed an hour but was still awake when she heard steps coming down the hall. The front doors were always wide open to invite any cooling breeze, so the firm sound along the passage was her first indication that Tim had returned.

It would have to be Tim with long, strong steps like that, but if so he had passed his own room and was stopping now at hers.

She slipped further under the sheets and lay very still. She waited for a knock. As the room was in darkness she decided it would be safe to feign sleep.

But there was no knock; instead, to her indignation, the door handle turned.

Tim came right into the room and right up to the bed.

'Don't play possum, missus,' he said, 'you're awake.'

For a moment Jessica was tempted not to respond, to remain prone so that he might think he had made a mistake, and go away. But on second thought she decided it might be wiser at least to have her eyes open.

She opened them and asked: 'What do you want? Don't you ever knock on doors?'

'Do married couples?' he drawled. 'I just wanted to tell you something.'

'Do you have to? Can't it wait until morning?' Jessica discouraged.

'It can, but I don't want you to toss around all night wondering what it was I had to say.'

'Very well,' Jessica sighed, 'say it.'

He loosened the neck of his shirt and sat on the bed. She withdrew as much as she could, but she could still feel the warmth of his body against hers, only a thin, summer sheet away.

'You didn't answer the phone tonight,' Tim said in the darkness.

'No, I knew it would be for you, so I switched through. Toby and Gillian had rung previously telling me their story.'

'Their marriage?'

'Yes.'

'. . . I suppose you told them ours.'

'No,' Jessica said.

'Why, missus?' he asked.

'Don't call me that!' she snapped.

'But you are. Ask Alf. Ask all the cattlemen. But if you don't like it, then why didn't you tell Toby and Gillian, *Jessie*?'

'Jessica. I could say I didn't tell them because it seemed unimportant, but actually they gave me no opportunity.'

'Fair enough,' he shrugged, 'but they know now, or if they don't they will very soon. I know my godmother.'

'Godmother?' Jessica asked.

'Yes, the ring was from her tonight,' he said.

'And you told her?'

'What will you say if I answer Yes, because *I* believe the news *is* important?'

'Did you tell her?' Jessica persisted.

'What will you say?' he persisted in his turn.

'I'll say you're lying, but go on.'

'Godmother rang to tell me she was coming

back to finish off the cookbook,' Tim announced.

'Oh, no!' Jessica objected. 'Not with . . . not with . . .'

'Two rooms in use?' He read her perturbation. Jessica could see his large white teeth showing in a wide smile in the darkness of the room.

'Yes,' she gulped. 'But perhaps' . . . hopefully . . . 'she need not know that we're—well—like that.'

'Like what?'

'. . . Married—but unmarried.'

'Oh, come off it—in the same house?'

'You should have put her off,' Jessica fretted.

'You try to put Godmother off anything she's set her heart on! She's set her heart on this cooking thing. She's determined to come back. So I told her.'

'Told her what?'

'About our marriage, but not our unmarriage, Jessie.'

'You're a fool,' Jessica said crossly.

'Not such a fool. I thought as I did so that we could extricate ourselves while she was here.'

'How?' she asked.

'A honeymoon,' he grinned. 'But I didn't get that far, Godmother beat me to it. After saying how happy she was for us, she asked me why we were here and not away, as newlyweds should be.' A pause. 'She's now booking us somewhere "suitable".' Again he grinned in the dark.

'This is all quite ridiculous,' grumbled Jessica. 'Gillian and Toby didn't go away.'

'They're away already. At The Alice.'

Jessica was still unsatisfied.

'You should not have left the booking to Mrs Reynolds. I hate these honeymoon places.'

'So you've been there before?' Tim asked.

Jessica ignored that.

'You could have let her come but told her that you were taking me around the country to see what goes on.'

'What do you think goes on?'

'You could have told her,' Jessica snapped.

'I could, and we could have done it, but I doubt if you would have approved of the accommodation. That consists strictly of only a one-man tent. You can't haul around too much, not on our tracks.'

'A one-man tent would have been acceptable,' Jessica stated.

'For two?' he asked.

He rose from the bed, but the thin summer sheet remained pressed down where he had leant against her.

'Anyway, like it or not, it's a honeymoon,' he said. 'I just thought I'd tell you—warn you about the knowing smiles, the flowers in the room, the rest of the business.'

'Charming,' Jessica replied, waiting for him to go.

He did not leave at once. He stood beside the bed, and in the darkness she looked at him, looked at the strong yet whipcord muscles showing beneath his shirt, the firm narrow hips, the powerful thighs. Unaware of doing so she relaxed the sheet she had drawn close around her, loosened and lowered it.

She waited for his next move, not speaking.

'Sleep tight,' he said, and went out.

After the door was closed, Jessica lay more sleepless than ever. The thought of a honeymoon hotel dismayed her—the extra attention, the permissive looks, the other newly-marrieds. She wondered if she could feign illness.

Then another thought occurred to her . . . and a much more disturbing one.

'You wouldn't have approved of the accommodation on the road,' Tim had said. 'A one-man tent . . . for two.'

But how many rooms, Jessica examined, could be expected in a hotel booking for a married couple?

More than one? she asked.

CHAPTER NINE

THERE were *two* rooms! Also a small hall! A sun balcony! Godmother had booked a very luxurious suite.

Even when Jessica had been helped into the Cessna, Jeff at the controls again, the stockmen out to wish them a happy holiday, she had not known where they were going.

In the plane, Tim had told her.

'The Barrier Reef. Been there before, missus?'

'No,' said Jessica.

'Well, I have, and I've always wanted to go a second time. See the Isle of a Million Birds again, the sooty tern, the wide-awake tern, the sheerwater and the noddy. The noddy, I must tell you, is a wonderful lover. He bows before his chosen mate, nods his head ... hence the name noddy ... and actually croons to her. Finally he offers his fancy girl the fish he has stored in his crop. Would you like me to court you like that?'

'Too late,' shrugged Jessica. 'I'm wearing a flower on the other ear, hadn't you noticed?'

'Showing you've got your feller.'

'I've got *a* fellow,' Jessica said. 'But no, I don't think I'd like that method of courtship. I don't mind the crooning, you have quite a good voice, but I wouldn't like the fish from your crop.'

'So you don't like fish?' he teased.

Jeff flew them all the way to Hibiscus Bay, a dreaming North Queensland town, full of banana palms and papaw trees, sibilant from the rustle of the canefields that grew right to its edge, and from the stir of the Whitsunday Passage.

Here they caught the island boat. Soon they were in the Passage, and Jessica, standing at the bow beside Tim, gasped at the sheer breathtaking beauty of this Barrier Reef. Everywhere there were islands, pine-clad islands, soaring steeply up to little peaks, islands surrounded on all sides with incredibly white sand. The sea around them was larkspur, the sky almost a postcard blue.

'Like your eyes,' Jessica said unthinking.

'My—— Don't tell me you know the colour of my eyes, missus,' Tim bantered.

'Well,' said Jessica, annoyed with herself, 'I know they're not brown or grey.'

'I don't know the colour of yours,' he told her, 'you never look at me.'

'They're pickle,' Jessica snapped.

'Show me.'

'Don't be silly, people will look.'

'If you glance around you'll know they won't look. They're most of them bound to where we're bound: a honeymoon hotel. They only have eyes for love. Have you eyes for love, Jessica? Let me see.'

She moved a few feet away from him, but he moved along with her.

'Show me,' he ordered, 'or people *will* be looking at us. I mean that, Jessie.'

With a stifled ejaculation Jessica turned and

stared fully up at him. He stared back. He stared until his own eyes became misty blurs to her, waving pools as intensely blue as the sea they sailed. Then:

'Yes, pickle,' he shrugged.

Though she had asked for it, Jessica was a little deflated. Her eyes had been described as autumn leaves ... Warm muscat ... a variety of pleasing things; pickle had been her own derogatory tag. Yet Tim was satisfied with it.

'Mustard pickle,' he elaborated. 'Look, we're nosing in.' He pointed to a small island with a long jetty. 'Summerwind Island,' he told Jessica, 'a new offering tourist-wise. A company has built a grand hotel.' He indicated a large white edifice, almost filling the entire island gem.

A miniature, candy-striped train was waiting to run them to the resort, and, leaving the boat, they alighted. In minutes they were there and being shown to their suite: An entry hall, a sun balcony ... *two rooms*.

Jessica smiled.

Though the smile was strictly to herself, she saw that Tim had noticed it ... that he knew the reason.

'Did you think it would be like the one-man tent?' he teased.

'I didn't think about it at all, really.'

'You damn little liar, you've been thinking about nothing else. You needn't have worried, Godmother Phyllida only ever goes in for the best.'

'Particularly in godsons,' Jessica said pertly.

'Of course,' he answered coolly.

'Well, this is a best,' admitted Jessica. 'It looks as though it was designed for a lady.'

'Excluding you, then,' he grinned. 'A lady is not my description of Miss Makin.'

'Mrs Fortescue. What is your description?'

'Woman,' he answered promptly. 'You're all woman.' A pause. 'That is, you will be—one day.'

Jessica did not answer. She put her bag on the bed . . . a large king-size bed. The bed in the next room was a divan type, and probably intended for a day lounge, she thought.

'Which bed do you want?' she asked as casually as she could. She did not turn round to him.

'It looks as though I have no choice.' Tim nodded to her bag. 'No matter, a cattleman can bed down anywhere. He has to.' He took his own bag to the smaller room.

They hung their clothes, then Tim suggested they go down for drinks. He could ring for them, he said, but under the palms in the garden seemed more attractive to him. He added that he had been about to say romantic, but had changed it to attractive. What did she think?

'I think a drink in the garden would be nice,' Jessica said.

'I meant attractive or romantic?' he persisted.

'A small squash with ice.' She ignored him.

'A long beer, no ice,' said Tim.

They went down.

After lunch they examined the coral through a glass-bottomed boat, pink, blue and violet coral, small bright fish darting between the starlike coral flowers. Tim bought Jessica a bunch of the coral from the hotel tourist shop. The bunch wore a tag: 'Handle with care. Like a heart this can break.'

'We mustn't have that,' Tim warned.

The hotel loudspeaker announced that a trochus lugger, unusually south in its search of shell, had moored near the western beach should anyone care to watch.

Tim and Jessica walked through the palm groves to the less frequented side of Summerwind to see the lugger lowering island boys into the translucent depths. Because it was only shallow water diving suits were not necessary, Tim said, but two minutes underwater was the limit.

They remained a fascinated hour, then spent another fascinating hour on the untouched side of Summerwind. Not so much white beach here, but interesting rock formation, a veritable maze of stony crevices and unexpected caverns.

Tim was intrigued with the pattern of the caverns, they seemed to honeycomb into each other. Jessica soon lost sight of him as he climbed down into one. She herself preferred surface to depth, so she went crabbing. It was fun watching the crabs pretend they were not there, then, if you came too near, go awkwardly off, but with a surprising speed in spite of their apparent clumsiness. Jessica was following up a large soldier crab when she heard Tim calling to her.

She followed the sound of his voice, but could not see him.

'Shout again,' she directed.

He did.

'I'm out of sight,' he told her. 'I'm down in one of the honeycombs.'

'That wouldn't interest me,' Jessica answered, thinking he wanted to show her. 'I don't like the underground.'

'It's not underground, it's under-cave, the cave I'm in is under another cave.' A pause. 'Jessica ——'

Jessica? He never called her Jessica. Something was wrong.

'What is it?' she asked at once.

'Possibly I could be trapped. The cavern was easy to get into, but I don't think it's going to be easy to get away from. How's the tide?'

Jessica looked to the larkspur water, and groaned.

'It's coming in.'

'I thought so.' Tim might have been passing the time of day, his voice was so unhurried. 'I think,' he said, still very composed, 'you'd better get advice.'

'Advice?' Jessica gasped, she had just seen an oncoming wave, and she felt sure it had gained a full five feet more than its predecessor.

'Advice on how to get me out,' Tim told her.

She glanced back to where the trochus boats were still operating, the onlookers still standing by. It would take ten minutes to bring them here, five minutes more for them to assess the position, and by then the position might be impossible. Even as she thought this another wave broke, and without any planning, any idea of what she was going to do, she ran to the gap from where Tim's voice had echoed, and jumped blindly in.

She landed on wet sand, not a good sign when Tim had called out that he was in a cave under a cave, but Jessica put that thought aside and looked around her for Tim's trap. It was not easy, there was a challenging labyrinth of caverns.

'Where are you?' she shouted. 'Where are you, Tim?'

'Where are *you*?' he yelled furiously back. 'You sound too damn near to me, Jessica. I told you to get help, not try to be heroic!'

'Advice was the word,' she corrected. 'I'm in the cavern above you and I'm coming down.'

'Bloody hell, stay where you are! Jessie, do you hear me?'

His voice came too late. Already Jessica was dropping down.

She fell into his arms, and she had never seen such an angry face in all her life.

'You damn idiot, you utter clown, of all the fools—as though one of us wasn't enough! Don't you see what you've done? You've trapped us both, but if you'd obeyed me, raised an alarm, there might not even have been one.'

'There would have been,' Jessica corrected, trying to match his composure but finding it hard. 'The tide is fairly racing in. I wouldn't have had time to alert anyone.'

'So you came to rescue me.' His face was still angry, but there was a seeking somewhere. 'Why would you do a dumb thing like that?'

'I didn't think of it as rescue,' she admitted.

'Then what?' he insisted, and the hands that had caught her tightened their grasp. 'What, missus?'

But Jessica could find no words. She only said incoherently: 'I just jumped.—Tim—Tim, *look out!*'

For a sudden wave was descending on them, it had broken over the top cavern and now was crashing down to the lower level. It was a surprisingly forceful wave, one of those occasional boomers that occur in incoming tides. This monster fairly filled the void with boiling, thrashing, swirling, smothering water. Then just as quickly and even more viciously it withdrew . . . taking them with it. Being slighter and lighter, Jessica passed through the aperture easily, but Tim had to use all his strength to get out. He also took a deal of battering, Jessica knew, by the bumping and scraping she could hear, by his grunts of apparent pain. But what did pain matter? They were the first words that were uttered when the two once more stood on the small beach, and it was Tim who said them.

'I couldn't see myself getting out of there,' he told Jessica. 'I might have been able to shove you through, but without the impetus of that wave I would have been trapped. By the way, have I thanked you for trying to save my life?'

'I don't want thanks. You see, I don't think I even intended a rescue,' Jessica admitted honestly.

'No,' he shrugged, 'and I expect as things are with us it would have been a neat ending.'

'Oh, don't be so dramatic,' she shrugged back. 'I simply followed when you jumped into the wretched cave. Well, you have your reward. Your head has a gash.'

'The honeymoon hotel will think we're fighting already,' he grinned. Then he asked: 'What was your reward?'

'Seeing you alive, I suppose,' Jessica said grudgingly. 'Also' . . . meanly . . . 'you're going to have a heck of a headache tonight.'

'Now that will be restricting,' he frowned. 'Something not done on the best of honeymoons.'

'Come back to the hotel and I'll patch you up.' She ignored his words. She went smartly ahead, but had to slow up for him. He seemed a little shaken, she thought, and slightly paler. Not his usual dark leather.

In the suite she got to work with warm water and bandages. The injuries were all on the top of his head where he had collided with a rock. She had to cut some hair away, but managed to drape other hair concealingly over the adhesive tape.

'Luckily you have a good crop of hair,' she told him, and then, impulsively: 'It's a wonderful colour—black, but with threads of dark red.'

'That's Inside Red. Every Centre man gets it. It dyes the skin, too. You'll have to watch your peaches and cream, missus.'

'Thank you,' Jessica accepted. 'I think that's the first nice thing you've said to me.'

'I said you were lovely on our wedding night,

recall?'

'You also added that it could be because of the dark,' she reminded him.

'Then I'll look into that again,' he promised. 'In the dark of tonight, missus.'

'Tonight you're going to bed with an aspirin,' she said firmly.

'Thank you, nurse, I can't wait. But before that exciting moment I'm hungry, so do you think I'll pass in the dining room or had I better ring for room service?'

'You'll pass,' Jessica assured him hurriedly. She knew dinner in the dining room would be by candlelight, for as they had gone by she had noted the prepared tables. But dinner in a large hall, even with candles, could never be as intimate as dinner alone, and intimacy she did not want, not in a confined suite instead of a large house full of rooms.

It was a good dinner. Tim praised the candles, but added that he missed the labels on the bottles. The following entertainment proved excellent. But after an hour of it he had had enough.

'I wonder if you're going to have a delayed concussion,' said Jessica as she helped him upstairs.

'I just have a hell of a headache,' he answered. 'Spare me the diagnosis and let me fall into bed.'

That suited her. She went into the bathroom and ran a bath, soaked luxuriously in it, then came out. By the time she went to the big bed, Tim was on the smaller bed, sleeping soundly.

She listened to his deep breathing a while, then went to bed herself.

She must have slipped off, for when his groans aroused her some time later she was too drowsy for a few minutes to establish where she was. Then she remembered, remembered what had happened this afternoon; she heard the groans once more, and began to piece things together.

She went out to the man on the divan and in the darkness found his pulse. It was satisfactory.

She put on the light and looked closely at him. He was still groggy from the wound he had suffered and the sedative she had administered, but otherwise normal, she judged. She decided that his painful groans were mostly being caused by the insufficient length of the divan, which was forcing his injured head against a wall. After all, the divan must only have been intended for day relaxation, and not for a bed; even for casual use it was much too short for a man of Tim's length.

'Tim,' she called, and she shook him gently. 'Tim, wake up! I'm moving you. You're going to sleep in the big bed, I am sleeping here. Every time you stir you aggravate that gash. Now get up and come with me.' She put out her hand.

He took it obediently, and let her assist him into the large bedroom. There he collapsed thankfully on the king size bed.

She slipped a pillow under his head, drew up a rug, and was just congratulating herself over a mission accomplished when she realised it was not accomplished at all. His hand holding hers did not lose its grasp.

She tried to disentangle herself gently, but when she found she could not delicately escape, she tugged. Tim still held tight—steel-tight.

Then quietly but progressively, still in semi-sleep, Tim drew her into the bed beside him, he steered her body to lie beside his.

Presently, relaxed by her warmth, he slept fully, and she let him. When he got very deep into sleep she would break away . . . really break this time. She doubted, in his almost drugged inertia, that tomorrow he would even remember.

An hour went past . . . probably two of them fled. Anyway, the music downstairs stopped.

Now Tim's breathing was very heavy. Stealthily Jessica started to slip away. But, almost cut off from him, he turned unexpectedly on her and anchored her. Then he drew her into the harbour of his arms. His body moulded her body. His lips found hers. A very long, very still moment went by.

Then Jessica felt him beginning to hold her even closer . . . then closer, and she knew with a sudden eagerness fired from his own eagerness that this hard, tough, all-the-way man was going to make her his wife . . . but no longer only in name.

She lay in his harbouring arms, not moving, almost beyond thought. She saw nothing but darkness with a dark face impressed on it . . . *but she felt his love.*

Then she heard his rhythmical breathing again, and with the measured sound of it reasoning came to her: the fact that what had just happened had been something apart to Tim, something in a dream state, not actual, never real, as it had been to her.

She got softly out and went to the divan bed. I'll watch him tomorrow, she thought, see if he remembers. But she was sure he would not.

She did not sleep herself. As soon as the first light buttered the sill of the smaller room she got up and found a mirror. She looked in it curiously, thinking to see a different face there, but the same face looked back at her.

Yet she *was* different, though only she . . . not he . . . knew it.

Knew she was a real wife now.

His. Tim's.

CHAPTER TEN

WHEN Tim wakened in the morning, he seemed considerably recovered, very refreshed ... but completely puzzled.

'How in Betsy did I get here?' He looked at the big bed.

But Jessica was looking at him, looking deeply. Bur finding nothing.

'Don't you remember that I changed our arrangement last night? she asked at last, watching covertly for a flicker of recollection. 'Don't you remember that I woke you up to tell you the divan was much too short for you?'

'It sounds rather dim to wake up a peacefully sleeping man to tell him he's too uncomfortable to sleep,' Tim observed drily. 'Are you sure that sleeping was your real reason?'

Jessica flushed vividly, and pretended sudden interest in something outside the window. *Her* only reason, she thought. If *he* only knew!

But if she had only known it Tim's eyes were focussed on her turned back. They were faintly laughing eyes ... they were quizzical ... but there was a searching there, too.

But Jessica's back remained turned.

'Well,' said Tim, 'if this arrangement suits you'

. . . he looked at the wide bed . . . 'it suits me. I do recall feeling slightly cramped on the divan.'

'Slightly!' Jessica left the window and came back into the body of the room. 'You were doubled up, your head was touching the wall.'

'It feels all right now.' Tim felt his head experimentally. 'During the night someone must have waved a magic wand.'

'Don't look at me,' Jessica avoided, 'I have no sorcery.'

'Only sauce,' he nodded, and went into the bathroom.

As he showered Jessica moved around the room, taking things up, putting them down again. Would he recall later, she wondered, or was it one of those things that once lost never return? Most of all, coming back to her former theme, how long could she go on like this? How long did he intend?

But she did not ask him, and he never broached the subject. They filled the day in very pleasantly, in the morning visiting Tim's remembered Isle of a Million Birds, in the afternoon exploring the outer reef.

They stayed up for the entertainment that night, even dancing several times. Tim was a good dancer, and seemed surprised that Jessica was surprised.

'All the Centre can dance,' he said. 'They cut their teeth . . . or should that be soften up their riding boots . . . on country hops.

Not at S.D., Jessica thought.

After supper they walked to the hotel beach.

Because the outer reef protected this side of the island the waves only rippled in. As the waves withdrew again there was a soft, sibilant wash.

It was a beautiful subtropical night, with a large gourd of a moon, a thousand silver stars. A night for honeymooners, Tim yawned.

Jessica looked at him covertly; in spite of his pertinent statement he seemed rather bored with the subject. Suddenly she wondered how he would react if she told him that—if she told him——

'I think we'll go back,' he said, yawning again. 'Now I've got the plum bed I'm anxious to see that no one challenges me for it.'

'Have no fear,' Jessica retorted. 'I'm comfortable where I am. Also, the bed is called king size, not plum.'

'Then see you pay homage.' The smile was edged this time.

Yet everything went smoothly, and the rest of the week in Summerwind Island was pleasant enough. If Jessica lay awake at night on the divan bed, staring through the window at darkness, wondering why sleep eluded her, wondering why she was wondering like this, the time still passed, and soon the week was over.

'Why is it always seven days for honeymoons?' Tim asked, watching Jessica pack her bag. His packing, which comprised throwing everything regardless into a suitcase, was finished, and he was relaxing back on a banana chair.

'Moon means a month,' corrected Jessica, folding busily.

'Yet only a week away together is called a honeymoon, proving the week must seem like a month,' he shrugged. 'In other words, goodbye to matrimonial honey.'

'You're always a cynic, aren't you?' Jessica said.

'Always,' he assured her. He got up and went to the window. 'One thing,' he remarked, 'the Isle of a Million Birds still grabbed me.'

'So it wasn't time wasted,' Jessica taunted him.

'No, missus, not at all.' He gave her a quick look.

They caught the ten o'clock boat to Hibiscus Bay, and Jeff was waiting on the small mainland strip with the Cessna for the flight to S.D. It was a lonely trip for Jessica. Anxious to check up on everything that had happened during his absence, Tim travelled beside the pilot, Jessica sat behind. It was only after they had landed, and Tim was driving the estate waggon that one of the stockmen had delivered to the home field for them, that she caught up with the news.

Gillian and Toby were settled down at Falling Star. Tim Browning had gone down to Sydney to visit his daughter. Godmother had arrived at S.D. the day after Tim and Jessica had left for Summerwind, and had gone again this morning.

'Very tactful of Phyllida,' Tim applauded.

'Very opportune for us,' said Jessica, but she did not feel the relief she had thought she would; the prospect of Godmother Phyllida, with her bright, busy, all-seeing eyes, no longer dismayed her, and she would not have cared if the old lady had stayed. She must have murmured this aloud, for Tim said shortly: 'Well, I would have cared.'

'Because your shares would have gone down with Godmother Phyllida?' Jessica queried.

'How?' he asked.

'*Two* rooms, and don't tell me that very nice but very busy busybody wouldn't have found out.'

'Yes, she would have found out, but my shares, as you put it, were going to plummet some time, weren't they?' He took his eyes off the track a moment to look narrowly at her.

'Yes,' she agreed coolly, 'so why not at once? Why be thankful that Godmother hasn't found out?'

'Because Godmother would have pestered me if the final break hadn't already been signed and sealed,' he told Jessica. 'I know that old woman. But now ... I mean later ... I can confront her with a fait accompli, a final decree. Too late for tears and persuasion.'

Jessica was silent for a moment.

'How much later?' she asked tentatively.

Tim shrugged. 'Your predecessors didn't break up the happy home for a year.' A pause. 'In other words, until after the child.' He looked sidewise at Jessica again. 'But that not being a consideration in our case, we're completely free agents.' Another pause. 'You agree?'

For several moments Jessica sat like stone. She pretended interest in the terrain, so different, she mumbled, to the coast. But Tim was determined on an answer.

'Do you agree?' he persisted.

'That we can break up at any time?' she asked.

'That without an issue, issue being the legal term for a kid, our position is vastly different. In fact' ... cheerfully ... 'we could even—get an annulment. Have you considered that?'

'Have—have you?' She tried not to stammer.

'Yes. But then I thought, how could I convince the powers-that-be that nothing ever had happened? I mean, of course, consummation, the natural conclusion. It would be simply my word ... and yours. What would prevent the powers-that-be from construing our replies as lies?'

'Nothing,' Jessica said as alertly as she could. 'In which case we'd better get out of it the usual way.'

'Agreed,' he nodded. 'You can name the time.'

'You have no thoughts yourself?' Jessica asked.

He answered cryptically. 'Oh, yes, I have.' But before she could question him they had arrived at the homestead.

Alf was very pleased to see them—also very proud of his news. Old missus had reported that she had found a magazine very interested in his bush recipes, and there was going to be a detailed article on him, photo and all.

'Celebration tucker tonight?' Tim anticipated when Alf had gone out again. 'Dinner by candle-light?'

'That's only for weddings,' Jessica reminded him.

'You mean no Drover's Dream? You mean

we've had our day?' Tim asked next.

She looked at him, irritated. 'Everything is always hopeless to you, isn't it?'

'On the contrary, I have a deal of hope.'

'Then I haven't,' said Jessica. Tim's words had puzzled and angered her. That 'hope' of his could only be his freedom again, she construed; he was free enough now, a man like Tim Fortescue would always be free, but he was not free on paper, and, being Tim, he would want that. She went down the hall to her room . . . but at the door she stopped.

The room was filled with flowers, with garden flowers, not dry, wild, Western ones. Silently Jessica thanked Godmother for the tribute, for it would have to be Godmother. She must have had them flown in from the coast.

She went across to the bowls and vases fairly spilling over with pansies, roses, poppies, all the lovely temperate offerings that could not be grown out here.

Better than his Salvation Jane, she sneered to herself.

She unpacked, then went down the corridor to ask Tim if she could unpack for him. She knocked on the door, then when he did not answer, she went in.

He was not there. He must have changed into his working clothes at once and gone out to join the men. Typical of him, he had rifled through his gear to find what he wanted, and his discards, and the travelling clothes he had also discarded, were in an untidy mess on the floor. It was time he took a wife. Then Jessica remembered that that was what he had done, and, in spite of herself, she laughed. What a husband I got! she thought, what an undisciplined, undomesticated brute. Just as well he's only a temporary brute.— How temporary? How long more for this deceit? 'You can name the time,' he had told her, but when she had asked him had he no thoughts himself, he had replied:

'Oh, yes, I have.'

What were those thoughts? she questioned. Was time running out even as soon as tonight? Tomorrow? Next week? Next month? Next year? But why wait like her predecessors had waited for a year? There was no child to be born.—Or was there a child? Suddenly Jessica stood very still. She remembered that night . . . and she wondered could there be such a night, could there be such a man, could there be a girl who had suddenly become a woman, and there *not* be something for remembering.

For an unguarded moment she cradled her arms around herself and swayed a little, then she gave an impatient shake, and, instead of tidying his mess as she had intended, she stepped over the pile of clothes and went out to Alf. In the kitchen she learned that the boss would be eating with the men tonight. It was Thursday.

She was asleep when Tim came home, so she did not hear his progress along the hall, she did not hear his tap on her door and his warning: 'Don't sleep too tight, missus, Jake Murphy has just reported to me that the wild horses have been sighted. If they're running this way tonight he'll alert me, and I'll take you to see them. It's a sight you'll never forget. How would you like a filly as an engagement ring, missus? More use than an opal?'

When there was no response, Tim went on to his room.

But at midnight he was in Jessica's room and shaking her awake.

'Up,' he ordered, 'time and horses wait for no man.'

'What on earth——' Jessica began crossly.

'The wild horses are running. That's something that has to be seen. Put on some clothes . . . anything will do. *No*' . . . as Jessica went to draw over only a wrap . . . 'more than that. I don't want my fellers seeing that much of my wife. Here, shove on these pants.' When she did not do it quick enough, he hauled them on her himself.

'Now *come*,' he demanded.

Outside the homestead there was an impatient posse of horsemen, all raring to go. One of them . . . Murphy, Jessica supposed . . . held two mounts, Tim's Sam, her Rebel. Tim legged Jessica up.

'Stick with the boys,' he said peremptorily, 'never wander away in the dark, or you could be lost all night; if you turned round a different rock, or brushed past a different stand of spinifex, you could be lost all the next day, all the next week . . . for ever.' He gave his Sam a light touch on the rump, a touch Sam did not need, for all the horses were drawing in long eager breaths, sensing something, fidgetting to start. Jessica's Rebel was sniffing the air.

'They're scenting the wild ones,' Tim nodded.

'Where are these wild ones?' Jessica asked.

'Murphy sighted them on his way up from Morning Star, he reckoned they were headed in this direction, but about four miles west. If we move fast we'll see them, and I'll get one for you.'

'Get one? You can't be serious! You can't take a wild horse,' Jessica protested furiously. 'You can't trap a wonderful, natural thing like that!'

'Brumbies are born for taming, the same as women.' Tim took his attention off riding for a brief moment to flick a glance at her.

But Jessica, for all her indignation, did not brood on that; it was taking her all her time to keep up with the stockmen.

They passed a rock outcrop she remembered from day gallops, a small clay pan, a stretch of gibber that was both distressing to the horses as well as the riders.

Then Murphy was indicating a rise in the flat terrain, calling to them to hurry because he could hear the wild ones coming. Even if he had not heard, their horses would have indicated it. They were pawing the ground, some of them were whinnying softly, one of them was rearing up and down in eagerness.

'Most of them . . . all of them, I would say . . . sprang from the wild ones,' Tim was telling Jessica quietly. 'They can't remember, of course, but they sense something, they sense old haunts, old hills, old days, old ways.' Then he said in a lit-up voice: 'Look, Jessie—look, girl!'

Jessica looked. She stared up to where Tim was pointing, and knew she had never seen anything like this before.

The wild ones were running. Small horses, tall horses, black, brown, bay . . . one glorious silver-grey. Dilated nostrils, flowing manes, shining eyes, sure, swift feet. They were passing by as in a film set . . . or in a dream sequence. They could have been as unreal as a film or a dream, except that the ground was trembling from their hooves. It seemed like a small earthquake.

Then . . . against her wishes, but what could she do? . . . Tim was eyeing the silver-grey, nodding to the native stockman Jimmy to cut the beauty out.

Jimmy, without his ten-gallon hat tonight, bareheaded, was whirling a rope, his fine dark brown eyes alight and excited. He sent the lasso spinning through the air, but the silver-grey veered at the final moment and the noose missed.

At once Tim was galloping with the wild ones, whirling a rope of his own. He spun it through the air and it caught the grey. There was a moment of threshing, of kicking, writhing and whickering, then the grey stood beaten while the rest of the mob went on.

'She's yours, Jessie.' Tim had come back to their own horses, leading the protesting grey girl. 'Better than that opal, don't you think?'

'Don't dare ask me what I think!' Jessica almost spat at him. 'You're outrageous, cruel, preposterous!' Her voice had risen, but she didn't care. She couldn't care if everyone heard.

But neither, it seemed, did Tim care.

'What's wrong with you?' he fairly yelled. 'I just told you all these fellers began as brumbies, surely you can see they're better off here with us. That mob you just watched is looking all right now, but it's not always like that. If there's no rain, and mostly there isn't, they go without food and drink, not like the boys and girls at the station, fed, watered, the rest of the thing.'

'But that's not it,' Jessica yelled back, 'they aren't cooped up.'

'At S.D. there are about three fellers to a paddock! Do you call that cooped up?'

'The wild ones are *free!*'

'So were you,' Tim shouted, undismayed by the frankly interested onlookers, 'until I took you in hand. By Harry, and I'd like to take you in hand right now! So you don't like my present?'

'No, I don't. I don't. I don't! I do——'

'I heard you,' he broke in, and he leaned over and gave her Rebel a slap to get going.

It was a light but crisp slap, and the smacking sound of it finished Jessica. She turned, her whip raised at him, but before she could act, Tim acted. He took her hand, forced her whip from her, then gave Rebel another prompting slap— not a hard one, the first had not been hard, either, but each had been telling, Jessica registered. Telling her.

The slaps had been hers.

'Both of those should have been administered

elsewhere,' Tim said clearly for all to hear. 'I'm only sorry it was Rebel who had to feel the weight of my hand.' A pause. 'But it won't be Rebel the next time, missus, so start moving. I'm towing the grey, so I'll take longer.'

He let her gallop off, but just inside hearing distance . . . hearing of everyone . . . he cupped his mouth impudently with both hands and called:

'Don't wait up for me tonight, Jessie.'

Jessica heard the barely-controlled rumbles of men's laughter as she continued riding back.

Aloud, she said nothing, she was far too embarrassed, but to herself she said bitterly: 'I hate him. I hate him! I hate him all the way, that hateful all-the-way man.'

CHAPTER ELEVEN

'I HATE him! I hate Tim,' Jessica said into her pillow for the brief remainder of the night. He's an overbearing, bullying, hectoring, inflexible tyrant, he rides rough-shod over everybody and everything, he's the king of these all-the-way men, these beef-makes-tough-boys gang, and I ... I'm his so-called wife.

So-called? A little voice in her asked and she twitched. She tossed in her large bed, hoping intensely that Tim was tossing in his narrow one. Tossing and turning, and not sleeping.

Morning came before she was ready for it. She would have loved to rest longer, but to do that would have spelled out to Tim that she had been disturbed last night, unable to sleep.

She took a long cold shower, then as well as the rub of lipstick which was all her clear skin needed, she put on some blusher.

She went to the kitchen. She would be out of luck, she thought resentfully, if Tim was there, for he always breakfasted much earlier.

But the boss was sitting at the big table in the eat-in kitchen. He had a large pot of tea at his elbow and he was munching a piece of toast.

He looked up as she put her head round the doorway, so there was no chance of silently withdrawing before he saw her.

'Good morning, missus,' he said.

'Good morning.' Jessica took a cup from the old-fashioned dresser that had never been replaced since Tim's grandparents' days.

'The tea is just made,' Tim said, 'and there's plenty for two. But if you want an individual brew, don't think of the expense.'

'It will do.' Jessica brought the cup to the table.

'Sit down,' he nodded.

'I'm not hungry,' she declined.

'And yet you look very healthy this morning, pink cheeks and all.' He looked quizzically at her. Did he ever miss anything?

'Sit down all the same,' he advised. He drew out a chair. He picked up a plate and served her her doorstep of toast. 'It can be cut smaller,' he informed her, passing her a knife.

'Thank you,' she said.

'Golden syrup?' he asked.

'No.'

'I would if I were you. Syrup is sweetening.'

'Naturally.' But Jessica knew he was not meaning sweetening for the toast, but sweetening for her. Why couldn't he leave her alone?

But he couldn't, it seemed.

Although she kept her eyes down, Jessica knew he was observing her.

'So you didn't sleep last night?' he asked her.

'What there was left of the night, you mean,' she snapped. 'Yes, I did.'

'Liar! In spite of those pink cheeks' . . . a small smile . . . 'you look like the morning after.'

'It is the morning after,' she said tightly, 'the morning after the worst night I've ever experienced.'

'Oh, come, the wild horses were a wonderful spectacle.'

'I didn't mean that.'

'Then I can assure you that last night was nothing to the nights we'll be having' ... he paused ... 'if you keep performing like this.'

'I perform! What about your recent performance? You made a fool of me in front of all your men!'

'What sort of fool would I have looked if I'd let you use that crop?'

'No fool,' Jessica said heatedly. 'After the way you bawled me out they would have agreed you had it coming.'

'Not them, missus—they know, as I know, that women have to be kept in their place.'

'It looks like it,' she sneered. 'Grovelling away from the female sex in this womanless waste. I don't want your tea. I don't want your barbaric toast!' She held up her slice, and it was fully an inch thick.

'Then what the hell do you want?' he asked.

'Out. I want to get out. You said to name the time. Well, I want now. *Now!*'

'No,' he said.

'But you told me——'

'Yes, I told you, but naturally I didn't think you would want to be exiting that quick. No, it can't be so soon, missus. Not until we visit your brother and Gillian, make sure there won't be any second thoughts there.'

'How could there be any second thoughts when they're married?' Jessica demanded contemptuously.

'*We* have second thoughts here,' he pointed out, 'and we have doubled up.'

'Doubled up!' she groaned. Did he always have to be so impossible? 'No,' she corrected, 'we had our second thoughts because we had no thoughts at all, something very different.'

'All the same, it's still not yet,' he ordered. 'I need more of the stockies to come to me asking about bringing their wives to S.D.'

'What?' Jessica disbelieved.

'There's a reason behind my insanity. When our final scene is staged, yours and mine, there'll be all the more disillusioned participants, all the more drop-outs. S.D. will be back where it was.'

'A desert . . . emotionally as well as physically,' said Jessica.

'In what way are you using physical?' he came in slyly.

A furious moment went by. Then:

'I'm leaving this place,' she told him with finality.

'How?' he asked.

'By your Cessna to Alice Springs, then the regular service to Sydney.'

'Paid for by whom?' he asked.

'By you. You promised me.'

'But I didn't promise you *when*. Oh, I'll pay for you, have no fears over that, but I reserve the right of an employer to choose the moment of sacking you, then settling up.'

'I'm pleased at least you didn't say the right of a husband!' she snapped.

'Now why should I say that,' he asked innocently, 'when I've never had any rights?' He looked hard at her.

She chose not to see the look, she took the dishes to the sink.

'Well, have I had any rights?' he persisted.

'Shouldn't you be able to answer that yourself?' she flashed.

'Sometimes, without knowing it, a man can walk in his sleep.'

'Oh, no,' she said, 'you've never walked in your sleep.'

'You put my mind at rest,' he smiled.

'There's another reason why you can't leave yet,' he resumed. 'It's Godmother. The longer we leave it, the less pressure there'll be from her.'

'There could be no pressure at any time from Godmother,' Jessica stated. 'I don't think she's ever liked me. And yet' . . . thoughtfully . . . 'she gave me all those lovely flowers.'

'Flowers?' he asked.

'My room was filled with them when I came home from my—when I came back,' she explained.

'They were not from Godmother, they were from me.'

'From you!'

'I thought it was the expected thing to do. Wasn't it? You see, I'd never done this caper before, never been married.'

'Caper?' echoed Jessica bitterly. After a moment she said stiffly: 'They were beautiful flowers. Thank you.'

'Better than Salvation Jane, would you say?'

'Than a noxious weed?—oh, yes!'

A few minutes went by. Jessica washed the dishes; she liked to have them done before Alf reported for duty. Alf was a very meticulous kitchenman, never a cup unwashed, never an item out of place.

Tim broke the silence.

'I'm sorry to disappoint you over your non-exit, your non-change after all from missus to ex-missus. But it has to be, Jessie. And in case you still feel like persisting, I'm not yet handing you your dues.'

'. . . If you ever hand them,' Jessica muttered.

'I give what I say I'll give,' he told her stiffly. 'For instance, I'm still giving you that ring.'

'But I thought you'd dropped that thought for a horse.'

'A filly. No, you're having both.'

'I don't want either.'

'You're having the ring and the filly. The filly is here, comfortably stabled, every want attended to. I think the least thing you could do is go and see her.'

'I saw her last night, and she's very beautiful . . . and very prisoned.'

'Are we going through all that again?' he glowered.

Jessica came right up to the table.

'Yes, we are—as one prisoner, because I am

that, aren't I?—I'm speaking out for another prisoner, because that prisoner, being a dumb
animal, can't speak for herself.'

'Which I wish you couldn't.' Tim got so vio-
lently to his feet that his chair fell back.

'You can tidy that, too,' he invited, and he took
up his wide hat and strode out of the kitchen,
then out of the house.

Several days later they drove across to Falling
Star. The young marrieds had changed it already
from rather bare bachelor's quarters to a pretty
domestic nook. The pair were rapturously happy.
If nothing else, Jessica thought, my coming to
S.D. achieved that.

'A good cattle couple,' were Tim's expected
words as they drove home again.

Jessica snorted softly, just enough for him to
hear. He let it pass.

Approaching the homestead, he said: 'We'll go
to Coober Pedy tomorrow.'

'Coober——'

'Coober Pedy. For your ring.'

'I'm not having a——'

'I'll fly you across at eleven hundred hours,
which is——'

'I know what it is, and I don't want a ring.'

'Eleven hundred,' he told her, halting the
waggon. As she slammed the door after her he
reminded her about the filly.

'She's settled in nicely for such a short time.
Have a look at her, get to know her, name her—
we can't call her "her" all her life.'

'Certainly it can't be Freda,' Jessica snapped.

'Freda, in my name book, means the obvious.'
She waited, then said: 'Free.'

'In my name book Freda comes from
Winifred,' he argued.

'A tough beef boy has a name book!' Jessica
sneered.

'An all-the-way-man does,' he corrected.

'Where does that connect?' she demanded.

'All the way with good old nature,' he pointed
out robustly. 'One day I intend to choose a name
for—a son.'

'Haven't you forgotten that a woman comes
into it?' she flashed.

'No, I hadn't forgotten,' he drawled. 'Had
you?'

She could not answer him for anger. She ran to
the open front door.

'Eleven hundred hours,' Tim called behind
her.

Jessica heard him leaving later for his office,
and she took the opportunity to slip across to the
stables to look at Freda ... no, not Freda, because the filly was a prisoner like she was. Two
Fortescue prisoners.

But if ever there was a captured animal less
imprisoned, Jessica had to admit privately, it
would be hard to find one, or to beat the silver
girl's conditions. The stable, in which she was to
be kept until she grew more accustomed to her
new life, the aboriginal groom told Jessica
proudly, was the size of four regular boxes put
together, and as each box, according to stable
rules, had to be fourteen feet by twelve, that

made Freda's home extremely capacious.

The manger was correct, too, breast-level, shallow enough for jaws not to be caught in it, deep enough to retain food. The wheat straw was bright, warm and fresh.

As for Freda——

Freda was beautiful. For a brumby she was quite astonishing. The stable boy said he had never handled such a contented wild one in his life.

When he moved away, Jessica put out her hand to the filly, and she saw that with a little persuasion the filly would actually have come to her. Already she could hear Tim's: 'I told you so.' She brought her hand down.

She bit her lip for a moment, then she said to the filly: 'Over my dead body is he going to domesticate you, you poor, wild, sweet thing.'

She went back to the house.

The next morning at the stipulated eleven hundred hours Tim flew Jessica to Coober Pedy.

Coober Pedy was the underground marvel of the West; because of the intense heat everyone lived underground, the shops were underground, even a church was at the bottom of descending stairs.

It was a bare, red, lonely town, an empty town while the workings were going on, but when the men emerged from their diggings for smoko, it became quite a hub. Because of Coober's isolation, visitors were always a diversion, and Tim and Jessica were smiled upon. Tim, noted Jessica, knew most of the diggers. She also noted that they treated him deferentially.

'Are you king here, too?' she asked him sarcastically.

'In a way all cattlemen are kings to diggers. You see, diggers have a tendency to dig, and if they dig, and don't fill in afterwards, a beast can break a leg, have to be destroyed. A cattleman doesn't care for that, and neither does a digger when he gets the account. We'll see Rolf. He has the best collection here.'

They went down a flight of wooden steps to a store, and it was wonderfully cool in the greenish light.

'It's cosy in the winter, too,' Rolf, a German, but many years here, assured Jessica proudly. 'What did you have in mind, Mr Fortescue?'

'Well, not diamonds,' Tim laughed. 'An opal ring, Rolf. Can we look around?'

Rolf bowed, brought out trays of rings, and while Jessica handled them, admired them, Rolf told her how an opal claim was a hundred and fifty feet square, and all that was needed was brawn and persistence. He shot Tim a look, smiled, and tacked on: 'Also luck.'

You had to dig, he admitted, then dig, then dig. There would be topsoil first, then sandstone, then the hard stuff that needed gelignite. But when you reached the opal, *if* you reached the opal, you certainly knew. It was like sinking your pick into glass, Rolf said, only you knew it wasn't glass.

'I like this one,' Tim broke in.

Rolf interrupted his account to look at Tim's

choice.

'That's Simpson's Strike,' he said in an awed voice. 'You're looking at a hell of a good ring, Tim.'

'It depends on the lady,' said Tim. He turned to Jessica. 'Does the lady like it?'

Did the lady like it? Jessica had never seen such a beautiful thing in all her life. It was the black variety, for Coober Pedy was black opal country, but Simpson's Strike was not black, for black opals were only called black to differentiate them from the pale specimens, it was flame, it was fire, it was sunrise and sunset, midnight and piccaninny light, all mixed together. The heart was a pure rose.

'Yes,' was all Jessica could murmur.

Tim slipped it on her finger and she could still say nothing.

But when Rolf brought along a velvet box she insisted on bedding it in there in spite of Tim's wish that she wear it immediately.

'Very wise,' said Rolf. 'Opals, like all gems, even diamonds, are not indestructible.' He cushioned the opal carefully.

There was a 'caff' at the Pedy; everybody, Tim told Jessica, spoke of the restaurant as the 'caff.'

'I'm leaving you there for a cup of tea while I do some business here,' he said.

'Rings for some of the tough boys for their wives they hope to bring out to S.D.?' Jessica dared.

'Not likely! No, a few debts I intend to collect. I have the names of a few itinerant diggers here who were grubbing previously at S.D.'

'They broke a few legs?' Jessica asked.

'Yes, and if they don't make good their care-lessness in not restoring a hole to its original form I'll break their legs.'

'So long as you don't break any hearts,' she said indifferently.

'I don't think I have so far. Have you? Or have you followed the advice attached to the coral I bought you at Summerwind and handled hearts with care?' He waited, then when she did not speak, he enquired: 'Is that coral still unbroken?'

'Unbroken,' she assured him. 'You could say—untouched.'

'Like your heart. I'll leave you here in the cool.' They had descended to the 'caff.' He placed her at a table and signalled for service. 'I'll be back in half an hour.'

Jessica sat drinking tea from a large pot and eating yellow slab cake. Alf would have snorted at bought cake, she smiled.

On an impulse she took out the velvet box and looked at the ring. It was glorious, so much so that it caught her breath. She became aware that the restaurateur was looking at it over her shoulder . . . and also catching his breath.

'That is some ring,' he said. 'That would cost a year's wages, I'd say.'

'How high a wage?' Jessica tried to laugh, tried to look unimpressed, for an idea she knew she should not consider, not for a moment, was occurring to her.

'A very good wage. You'd get a good price for

that.'

About to answer that a good price had been paid for it, she refrained.

'Is Rolf the only opal seller?' she asked casually.

'Oh, no, there's Hendrik, there's Ambrose, they're dealers as well.'

'Dealers . . . you mean they buy as well as sell?' Jessica asked.

'Yes. Would you like a jug of hot water to top up your tea?'

'No, thank you, it's been most refreshing. I think I'll have a stroll around.'

'It's cooler underground,' the restaurateur advised, 'but upstairs you might always kick over some potch.'

'What's potch?'

'Discarded stuff from the diggings, quite worthless, but sometimes pretty. Tourists think they've picked up a fortune.'

'Very well then, I'll go after potch,' Jessica smiled, and got up.

She climbed the stairs, but she did not walk towards any of the diggings, instead she went underground again, but to another section.

The sign on the shop she surreptitiously entered read:

Ambrose. Selling. Buying. Best prices given. Under it in big letters was Opals.

When Tim returned in half an hour she was waiting for him. The first thing he did was pick up her hand and look at her finger.

'Still not engaged?' he asked.

'Only married,' she answered. 'Simpson's Strike is safe in its plush coffer.'

She was not actually speaking an untruth, she appeased herself, for unless Ambrose had taken it out, the opal still fired, flamed, glowed and flowered in a small velvet box. And rested in a cool cavern.

CHAPTER TWELVE

SEVERAL times in the following week Tim asked Jessica why she was not wearing Simpson's Strike.

'It's too valuable,' Jessica always evaded.

'It's for wear, not stare,' he said. 'I want it aired, not stowed away.'

After several similar observations he made no more comment on her left hand that wore only a plain gold band, for Jessica could not summon the nerve not to wear *that*.

She suffered great waves of shame over what she had done. How could she have gone to another opal dealer and sold the ring for less than what Tim had paid for it? For it would have to be less, a profit would need to be made.

But she still had done it, and, for all her guilt, Jessica still felt it had been her only course. Tim had refused to hand her her exit money ... she called it that now ... and though she knew that he was a strictly reliable man and would keep his promise in the end, she needed that promise to be kept immediately. She wanted to leave S.D., leave Tim. In short she wanted Out. At once.

She did not know why she felt so urgent about it, and she did not care to analyse the obsession, for an obsession it had become, she only, and blindly, wanted to get away before—well, before it was too late.

Too late? Why had she said that?

Several wives had arrived at Saffron Downs, and small but sufficient prefabs had been supplied to them. For the first time in three generations the canteen had male *and* female customers. There was even a little child toddling around, and there was an obviously pregnant young wife.

Jessica had refused to discuss the mother-to-be with Tim when he had asked how long the M.T.B. should remain at the Downs before she was transferred to the Base.

'Hell's bells, you're a woman,' he had burst out when she had declined . . . he was very irritable lately . . . 'so give me some womanly views.'

'In her condition my views would be rather late,' Jessica had answered coolly.

'Meaning you don't like children?' he had chosen to interpret.

'I never said that. I do like children. I simply meant that very obviously any views now would be redundant . . . superfluous.'

'Because she is as she is?' he persisted doggedly.

'Pregnant? Yes,' Jessica answered.

'And from a man-hater, like you are, if she had had any sense she wouldn't be?' he chose to interpret further.

'Your words,' Jessica had told him, and had started to turn away, only to be caught and turned back again, then held firmly.

'So easy to be glib about others when one is confident one is not "that way" oneself,' he had suggested with deliberate inelegance. 'So disburdening to be sure' . . . a pause . . . 'even cocksure.' He had raised one malicious eyebrow at her, and Jessica had felt a sudden inquietude . . . *even a doubt*. How deep into that dream state had Tim been that night?

'Thanks for the un-advice,' he had finished. 'I'll pass on to Evie that Missus couldn't care less.'

'Yes, tell Evie that.' Jessica had taken the opportunity of a loosening in his grasp to escape.

She had gone out to the stables . . . or rather to the grey girl's stable. Even though Jessica had not sought the filly's favours, the silver beauty was coming right up to her now whenever she called there.

'You're very lovely,' Jessica told her today, 'and obviously being treated as you deserve, but you're still a prisoner, a prisoner like I am.' Only that morning Jessica again had told Tim that she wanted to leave, and again he had demanded: 'How? Your journey paid for by whom?'

'But I have to go, darling,' Jessica said to the filly. 'If I don't go I'll be trapped—trapped by something I can't fight, because I don't know what it is, and because I've never known it before. All I'm really aware of is that I must get away.' She looked at the filly thoughtfully. 'We both could get away, you know, you through me, I through you. If I let you out now, you would be a prisoner no more, then Tim would be so angry with me, because he would know who did it, that I would be away almost on your heels. Yes . . . on your heels . . .' As she was saying it, Jessica was unfastening the barn door. It was rather an anticlimax when the filly did not gallop out at once, but eventually, after some shooing, she did. Only several moments afterwards the stable hand returned.

But Jessica, too, was gone by then; she was in her room waiting. She had no doubts that Tim would guess what had happened instantly, so she braced herself in preparation.

But nothing happened . . . not for several hours.

The stableboy, understandably, had looked for the grey mare first, looked very thoroughly, then after that alerted the other boys to look with him, and they had all gone out on their horses.

Only when things loomed really black did they finally find Tim, tell him, and Jessica could imagine how black everything would be then!

Yet when he came to the house for dinner he was more puzzled than angry.

'I'd stake my life on Andy,' he said, 'I'd swear he wouldn't leave a stable door open.'

'Did he?'—How could she act like this? Jessica wondered.

'Well, the filly's gone,' Tim said.

'The grey girl?'

'Yes, the wild one, who else?'

'It could have been the door catch,' said Jessica. She had not meant to take this stand, she had meant to admit her blame right from the first, get bawled out for it, then finally, furiously, irrevocably dismissed, at last allowed to leave,

turn her back on S.D. for ever. Yet facing up to
Tim in thoughts was very different from facing
up to Tim in reality, she found.

'The door is perfect,' Tim frowned. 'No, it had
been opened, then left open, something no doubt
that you often considered.' He looked witheringly
at her. 'You must be very pleased with yourself
that your wishes have come true.'

'No ... no ... I'm not pleased,' Jessica said
unhappily, disappointed in herself that she felt so
dejected suddenly, and not the dejection of the
wrath that Tim soon would be heaping on her
but the dejection of an empty stable, an absent
filly.

So much for the freedom bit, she thought.

'Well, Andy is for it,' Tim said briskly.

'For it? You mean ... what do you mean?'

'Oh, I'm not going to lash him, thrash him,
send him back to the mission, expel him back to
his tribe, but I am going to cut his pay packet
down, demote him to cleaning the stables again,
which will be the worst hurt of all. He loves the
close contact of horseflesh. If his sole relationship
with it is cleaning up only, it will be a very hard
lesson.'

'But why inflict it when he didn't do it?' Jessica
begged.

'The stable was Andy's responsibility and the
door was open. What other evidence do you
want?'

'Someone else might have——' Jessica began
to stammer.

'Name of?' Tim demanded harshly.

It was no good, Jessica realised; he would have to know it in the end, so it may as well be now.

'My name,' she said in a small voice.

'Name of?' he repeated, thinking she was trying to be funny.

'Jessica Makin—*Fortescue*,' she said clearly.

He did not believe her for a long moment, and then his belief was thin.

'Stop trying to protect the boy, stop being heroic,' he told her.

'I'm telling the truth—I opened the stable door, I let the filly out. She wouldn't go at first, I even had to clap my hands.'

'I could clap you in irons,' he muttered, real belief in what she was saying slowly sinking into him. He moved back from her, then left the room.

He was soon back again.

'You actually *mean* this, Jessie?' he shouted.

'Yes,' Jessica said.

'Tell me why? Give me one reason why?' he demanded.

'There is only one. She was a prisoner.'

'You fool, you utter little idiot, don't you see what you've done?' He glowered across the room at her.

'Yes, I see. I've freed her—and don't try to tell me that horses are like birds, and that when one of them returns to the others, the others reject it.'

'No, I'm not telling you that, because none of them ever return. How could they . . . all those miles away?'

'But in time——' Jessica began nervously.

'In that time the mob, too, would be further away. What did you expect they would do? Stand around and wait? It's most unlikely that the filly will ever rejoin them, ever see them again. Wild horses seldom double up on their tracks.'

'Then—then what will happen?' Now Jessica's lip was trembling.

'The grey girl will have to look around for food, for drink, for a sheltering place from the hot sun during the day, a place to sleep at night—rather difficult when you've been catered for, even cosseted, before "freedom" took over. Also, she's young, not used to being alone, not used to coping alone; prior to Andy she had the older, wiser mob around her, now she has only herself. Think on that, Mrs. Freedom Marcher!'

Again, in disgust, he went out. But once more he burst back.

'There must be another reason why you did it,' he said to Jessica, 'some personal one. It wasn't just the filly.'

'No,' said Jessica, 'it was my freedom, too. I—I felt myself in the same position as the grey.'

'I think you mean you became the grey?'

'I suppose so . . . in a way. But what I really meant was we were both fenced in. The filly was—I was. So I thought if I released her you would be so disgusted with me that you would—would open my door, too.' She looked appealingly at him.

He stood looking back at her a long moment. Then:

'No way, ' he said definitely.

'But——'

'No way. At least not until I'm ready.'

'When will that be, Tim?' she asked.

He shrugged.

'But this is all a fiasco,' Jessica cried. 'Why do we have to keep on with it? You're free of whatever threatened you before, so let me go away to lead my own life, let you lead yours.'

'No,' he refused. 'It's not over yet. You have to stay a while longer, until the final disagreement we stage is *so* emphatic, *so* unarguable, *so* impressionable, *so* much the point of no return that this ridiculous position we have here now topples. Topples for all time and for everyone to see.'

'But this episode could be it,' she urged eagerly. 'You could tell your men what I did, what an inferior, abject *woman* did—stockmen care for their horses much more than women.'

Tim shook his head. 'It could be that they do,' he stated, 'but I want more than horseflesh for an argument, more than a deliberately opened stable door to state my case.'

'So?' Jessica breathed.

'So *I* will say when the topple comes,' he told her, 'not you.' He looked at her narrowly. 'You understand?'

'No, I——'

'*You understand?*'

'Yes.'

Jessica turned and went to her room.

Oh, yes, it was understood by her, she thought grimly, understood that by this time tomorrow she would have left Saffron Downs, come hell or high water she would have gone for ever. She could stand it no longer. She could stand Tim no longer. She was exiting on her own accord, and nothing, and nobody, would stop her.

But before that could happen she had to find her escape.

She had her money ready. Since she had sold the opal the notes had been concealed in the bottom of her wardrobe. Now she knelt down and counted them again. There was sufficient, and much more, to fly her down to Sydney. Her only trouble was whom to ask about a flight.

No use to try to bribe Jeff, the young pilot; he would never have deceived the big boss. Ever since the ceremony in Tim's office Jeff's attitude to her had changed from admiration to respect— respect for *Mrs* Boss. So Jessica dismissed Jeff.

But there must be some chartering men out here, probably Alice Springs could provide some. Once she got to The Alice she could take the regular service south.

She found a telephone book and studied it, made a note of several numbers.

The next morning, after Tim had left, and before Alf came on duty, she rang.

The first number could not do the job, the second said it could, but only from a place unknown to Jessica called Stump Hollow. She drew a brave breath and accepted the charter without query.

She gave her name as Jones. It could have been Smith, she just said the first thing that came to her mind. Yes, she said, that price would suit her.

She heard Alf arriving, and went out to see how successfully she could pump him as to the location of Stump Hollow. She had thought it better not to plead ignorance to the pilot, she had already found that here in the West things got around very quickly: even a wind could carry a secret. Tim had said that once.

If she had admitted to the charter that she only knew Saffron Downs, they could have passed on that interesting snippet to someone else; she could have encountered someone very unwanted out at this Stump Hollow, wherever it was.—Yet would that have happened, Jessica wondered, in spite of what he had decided would Tim be as glad to be rid of her as she was to go?

She went into the kitchen, ostensibly for coffee, perching cheerfully on the stool. She chatted unimportantly to Alf, among other things saying what a fine young pilot Jeff was, asking Alf did he only do S.D.'s work.

Alf said Jeff did, but that there were several charters for people who had call for them.

'But are there any suitable fields around?' Jessica asked slyly.

'Billington's, Lucy Bank, Stump Hollow,' said Alf.

'That's a funny name,' Jessica commented. 'Is there really a hollow?'

'Flat as a billiard table,' Alf told her. 'It's just off our west road, no distance at all really. I thought steak again, missus, what do you say?'

What did she say? It was always steak, except when it was a wedding banquet, then it was

Drover's Dream.

But Jessica was not thinking of weddings now, she was thinking eagerly: Off the west road . . . no distance at all. She could have kissed Alf. Instead she said: 'Yes, steak.' She drained her coffee and strolled out.

But once in the passage she hurried to her room and put a few things in a small bag. When she went she would take the car and leave it there at the strip. You could leave anything here forever and not have it touched.

She would write to Tim from Sydney when she got there, tell him what she had done, tell him to collect the car and—and fix up getting unmarried. (She found she could not call the process anything else but that.) She would say she would agree to anything he wished. All she wished was what she was doing: dropping out.

The charter was bringing in a party to Stump Hollow, the voice over the phone had instructed Jessica, so if Miss Jones could be at the strip mid-afternoon—

'I'll be there,' Jessica had promised.

The hours seemed endless. Now that she had started action, action could not come fast enough. She went from room to room, filling in time.

She was relieved when Tim did not appear for lunch, when Alf went across to the barracks for his customary catnap which he always took in the early afternoon and thought nobody knew anything about.

She took up her bag, went out to the car, drove off to the strip. She had plenty of time; she had

assured herself of that in case the location of the
strip eluded her. But it did not. She found it at
once, in fact she wondered why she had not
noticed it before. She parked the car under a
raggy gum, leaving the keys on the seat.

She waited.

After half an hour she heard the distant whirr
of a small craft. Minutes later the plane appeared,
a more capacious one than Jessica had thought,
larger, anyway, than Tim's. It taxied along the
flat, sparse, yellow grass, then the engines cut.

As the door opened there was the sound of a
car joining her car . . . no, looking around, it was
an estate waggon. It was Tim's! Tim was getting
out! But he was not looking at her.

He was approaching the group leaving the
charter, he was going forward to greet them.
There were six young men and one woman, Jessica registered, an elderly woman.

It was Godmother.

CHAPTER THIRTEEN

THE odd thing . . . to Jessica . . . was that nobody seemed at all surprised to see her there.

The men presumably accepted her as having driven out to meet them. It was the same with Godmother Phyllida, who kissed her, then introduced a press photographer and a press journalist, a television cameraman and a television journalist, a publisher and his reader. 'Like your Alfred, also a cook,' Godmother whispered of the reader as she made the presentation.

The other member of the small assembly, the one who had come out in the waggon, did not show surprise, either, but Tim could be very inscrutable, Jessica thought.

Godmother was chatting busily; she thrived on happenings.

'When I wrote to Timothy telling him Alfred's news and saying we were coming I told him to keep it as a surprise,' Godmother Phyllida said, 'but of course he would tell his own wife.'

'Of course.' Tim was standing by Godmother's side, but still not looking at Jessica. 'The important thing is that I didn't tell Alf.'

'Dear Alfred,' Godmother beamed, 'I wonder how he'll take all this.' She waved to the men, the cameras, the notebooks, the portable typewriters, the microphones.

'He'll love every minute,' Tim assured her. 'I can see him on television ... not the Galloping Gourmet but the Country Cooky, or the Beef Bushie, or—What name do you suggest, Jessie?' Tim actually turned for the first time since he had come to the strip and looked directly at Jessica. His eyes were blue ice.

But he looked back to Godmother at once, and Jessica heard him telling her why he had recommended the charter. It was because his own smaller Cessna could not have accommodated six passengers and all that equipment, for larger cameras and screens were being taken off the craft. Suddenly remembering why *she* was here, Jessica saw the pilot getting off as well ... looking enquiringly around the field ... looking around for his passenger, she knew. For a giddy moment she wondered if she could step forward after all, climb into the plane, go through with it all. She even took a tentative step.

As if he had read her thoughts, Tim brushed her back with a seemingly casual ... but telling ... arm. Then he went across the field himself. Obliquely Jessica saw him talking to the pilot, then she saw him reaching into his pocket.

A few minutes later the charter left.

Tim returned to the group, directed the loading of his waggon with the equipment and the men, then waved Godmother across for Jessica's care. But he preceded the old lady to the little car to open the door for her, and in the moment before she got in he said in a low voice to Jessica: 'Wipe that terrified look off your face, missus,

I've paid *Miss Jones's* account.'

He helped Godmother aboard, and slammed the door.

So much for Stump Hollow, Jessica thought bleakly as she followed the waggon back to the homestead. She wondered if she would ever come out to it again.

But if she was bleak, Godmother was in high spirits. She confessed to Jessica that she loved missions, hence her stay here recently at S.D. with little Gillian, and hadn't *that* mission turned out wonderfully, Jessica dear? The pair were made for each other.

Her mission now was Alfred. The publishing firm to which she had gone with his bush recipes had been so impressed that as well as accepting the collection they had wanted to interview the cook. At her suggestion they had decided it would make more interesting reading and better viewing if the sequences were set at S.D. itself.

'Also you had to be in it,' Godmother went on busily.

'Me?' Jessica was startled.

'You and Timothy. Saffron Downs is such a large place. A quarter the size of Texas, I'm told. Much bigger than anything in England.'

'But where do I come into it?' Jessica asked again. 'Where does—Tim?'

'The romantic angle, dear. An old house becoming a home after all these years. People love things like that. We'll entwine them around Alfred's recipes.'

Jessica gulped.

But as she followed Tim's laden waggon to the homestead, she stopped gulping and began frantically trying out her arithmetic instead.

There were eight bedrooms at the house, but here were nine people . . . including the Fortescues . . . to be fitted into the eight rooms, and——

And nine into eight did not go.

But perhaps the men could cross to the barracks . . . or sleep on the verandahs.

'They'll all sleep in the homestead, Alfred.' Godmother was saying some ten minutes later to a surprised and excited Alf, and she directed him to bring out the necessary linen.

'You help him, dear,' she ordered Jessica. She called out to her godson: 'I am right, am I not, Timothy? Even though the old house has forgotten hospitality it will soon remember.'

'It hasn't forgotten,' Tim returned.

Alf was so elated he could scarcely handle the sheets and blankets, and in the end Jessica suggested that he return to his kitchen. After all, he had six more to cater for tonight.

That did not worry Alf, he loved a challenge. But he was concerned whether it should be a beef dinner or mutton.

'Drover's Dream,' decided Jessica for him. 'Get going, Alf.'

'Thank you, missus,' grinned Alf, and left.

Jessica proceeded absently with the bedrooms. She was in a kind of drover's dream herself. She wondered what the boss drover was doing . . . when she could expect to be bawled out, for that, she knew, was inevitable. But what still was worrying her most was her arithmetic. Nine into eight definitely did not go.

The media dragged Alf from his kitchen to take some shots of him, before dark set in, mixing a bush damper. Godmother followed them to add her advice.

For the first time since it had been descended upon the old house stood silent.

Jessica finished the current room, then, laden with equipment, struggled down the hall to begin the next one. She had barely made it before she heard Tim's steps starting the long trek from the front door to the back. She knew those steps by now. She should do, she thought, they had come . . . *and stopped* . . . often enough. But if she remained silent now they should come and go, not stop. He would not know she was here, and her 'bawling out' would have to wait until later. Even though it was inevitable, it was better postponed. She stood, still linen-laden, behind the door.

For a moment she thought she had succeeded, then the handle turned, and he came in.

'How did——' Jessica began crossly.

'How did I know where my wife was?' he finished for her. He took the linen from her and got on one side of the bed to be made up, indicating for her to get on the other side.

'When it's you, Jessica,' he told her, 'I can see through walls.'

'Evidently also see through me,' Jessica suggested. 'How did you know I was leaving Saffron Downs?'

'I didn't know,' he admitted. 'I simply went

out to pick up the crowd, that was all. But' ...
straightening a sheet with more than necessary
firmness ... 'I knew then.' He added grimly:
'Miss Jones.'

He waited for a few moments, punching a
pillow into shape as he did so, then he burst out:
'Why in damnation did you do such a bloody
thing?'

'As what?' Jessica dared.

'As ringing up for a charter. As thinking you
could leave me.'

'I was going to send any money left over back
to you,' she assured him. 'I considered I was
entitled at least to a fare.'

'Not so fast,' he broke in. 'The money left over
from what?'

But Jessica found she could not answer that,
not yet, so instead she persisted: 'You did promise to pay my way back.'

'Yes, I did,' he told her slowly and deliberately, 'in spite of the fact that at no time did I
have any real intention of standing by it.'

'What?' Jessica disbelieved. If nothing else,
and there had been nothing else, she had thought
of him as a man of honour.

But—now?

'I was dishonouring that promise even as I
uttered it,' Tim went on, 'because I knew that
soon I had no hope in Hades of ever ridding myself of you.'

'But——' Jessica blurted, 'what——'

'You came into my life uninvited,' he said
doggedly, 'and then you set to and started a

whole procession of things I thought I never wanted, things I believed I despised, things I had prevailed upon others to despise as well.'

'You mean your well-trained woman-haters?' Jessica asked. 'Your tough beef boys? Your all-the-way men?'

'There are other ways to go all the way,' he said quietly. 'I found that out, Jessie.'

'Yes,' said Jessica. She stopped herself from reminding him: 'You made me find it out, too.'

Instead she probed: 'What were those things I started?'

'Things like home.' He looked around him. 'Like wives.' He looked at her. 'Like——'

'Like life.' Jessica slipped that in, in spite of herself.

'Yes—life.' He looked at her deeply, but she avoided the look.

He waited a moment, then he left his side of the bed and came round to her side. But he did not come up to her.

'I fought against it,' he told Jessica. 'I fought as hard as I knew . . . as hard as I could. But' . . . a shrug . . . 'I know when I'm defeated.'

'*You* know defeat!' Jessica disbelieved.

'Yes, Jessie.' Now his voice came in a lower key, a softer key, if this man could ever be soft. 'I know I'm defeated when an old tree blossoms. Look at this place, it's flowering.' He gazed around him, then:

'You are the flowering,' he said. A pause. 'You are my flower.' He stopped talking but kept looking at her.

Jessica stood bewildered. She did not know this *different* man.

'I sold the opal,' she blurted miserably.

'And got damn less for it than you should have, you little fool' The difference was gone, he was Tim again.

'You knew?' Jessica asked.

'That same day. You don't know our West yet. You don't know that what I'm saying to you right now is already being discussed as far as the Northern Territory. We have bush telegraphy here. There's nothing secret.'

To her dismay Jessica heard herself stating: 'Two beds were.'

'They can't be secret tonight,' he stated back. He gave a wry smile and added: 'Nor sacred. Not with nine in the house.'

She sat down on the still unfinished bed.

'Couldn't the men go across to the barracks?' she asked.

'No,' said Tim.

'Couldn't their beds be pushed out to the verandahs? We have four verandahs.'

'No,' Tim said again.

'Does hospitality matter all that much to you?' she tried next.

'It does now. Also, missus, you're forgetting Godmother. That woman has eyes in the back of her head.'

'Then does Godmother matter?' Jessica persisted.

This time Tim said: 'Yes.'

But still Jessica tried . . . she had to.

'It was different on Summerwind,' she pointed out, 'we had a suite there.'

'With two beds,' he agreed calmly. 'Tonight there will only be one.' He paused, and it was a very long pause. 'But only one needed, missus, the same' . . . another and even longer pause . . . 'as—*there*.'

'As there?' Jessica sat staring up at him. At last she moistened her lips.

'You knew?' she whispered.

He nodded.

'You were not asleep, or concussed, or——'

'No,' he assured her, 'not at all.'

'You—you were laughing at me!' she cried.

'No, by heaven, I was *wanting* you, Jessie,' Tim cried back. 'I've been wanting you ever since. I want you now. But' . . . stepping back . . . 'I can wait.' Without another word he left.

In a daze Jessica finished the beds. Then she went down the hall to the big room with the one big bed. She lay down. She shut her eyes.

She understood now why she had tried to get away from S.D. It was because she had felt she was being trapped. But what she had discarded was the *knowledge*, not just a feeling, that she was intended to be trapped, intended to remain here, intended to be Tim's all the way wife, not no-way as it was now. At last she had recognised that fact, accepted it. Now she was even embracing it, wishing eagerly that he was here to embrace *her*.

She knew she wanted him for ever, not only for a year as the other wives had lasted, not only until the child was born.

The child!

She got up from the bed to stare at herself in the big mirror. It was a long, searching, wondering, incredulous stare that slowly, breathlessly admitted credulity.

Our child, she thought.

'You're a rose,' Tim said from the doorway. 'You're glowing. You know what that means, don't you, missus? It means you're in bud. As a cattleman, I know productiveness.'

This man was outrageous! Half laughing, half indignant, she told him so, but he only retorted: 'Hell, Jessie, you didn't think, did you, there could be such a night and not something as a reminder?' He laughed at her.

Jessica flushed and defended: 'But I'm not cattle.'

'No,' he agreed.

He came across to her, pulled her close to him, ran his fingers through her hair, moved his hands over her shoulders, traced her backbone up and down, touched the hollow of her throat, cupped her breasts, kissed her lips. There was a hunger in his eyes that Jessica knew must mirror the hunger in hers.

She glanced to the window where darkening had barely begun, and Tim looked after her.

'There's a few hours yet between now and then ... and us,' he said quietly. 'There is also,' he added, 'a Drover's Dream dinner to eat ... shots of Alf ... shots of the newly-married Fortescues ... the rest of the stuff. Did Godmother tell you?'

'Yes,' said Jessica.

'Well, I thought that when you got prettied up for the cameras you might add this.' He handed her a remembered velvet box.

'You bought the opal back again!' Jessica cried.

'For much more than the first time, you idiot,' he glowered, 'so see you wear it, or else ... Two other things, Jessie,' he added.

'Yes, Tim?'

'I noticed that the coral was broken. You were warned that coral broke like a heart.'

'It wasn't broken when I saw it last,' she said.

'Well, it is now. I was looking for the opal and must have smashed it. Does that mean I've broken your heart?'

Jessica ignored him. 'Why were you looking for the opal when you knew already from your bush telegraphy?' she demanded.

'I couldn't believe you would do it,' he said simply, 'so I searched.'

'In my room!'

The devilish eyebrow shot up at her.

'What was the other thing, Tim?' Jessica asked him.

'The filly. Freda came back. Andy found her at the stable door waiting to get in. A *willing* prisoner—Miss Jones.'

'I'm glad she's back,' was all Jessica said.

'I'm glad *you* are,' Tim said quietly. Just as he had before, he turned and left.

Jessica dressed. She put on the ring. She went out to the big dinner in the big dining room. She was interviewed with Tim, she was photographed with him.

'It would look rather silly now, wouldn't it?' Tim slipped that in when he found an opportunity.

'What would look silly now?' Jessica asked.

'A topple. Remember me saying I wanted all this to topple? Well, the only real topple, Jessie, was Fortescue for Makin. That was one hell of a topple. Damnation, when is this night going to end?'

The night did . . . at last.

Alf went across to the barracks. The six men went to their six rooms. Godmother went to hers.

Tim extinguished the final light of the homestead; when you had to depend on your own plant you needed to conserve. Besides, he pointed out, who needed light?

Jessica, lying in the darkness, heard the long loose steps coming along the long dark hall. They were coming unerringly to the master bedroom where before only missus had slept.

But two would sleep there tonight . . . tomorrow night . . . all the nights. Why, Jessica discovered, I can't hear his steps for my heart!

The door was opening and the all-the-way man was coming up to the big bed.

'Did I tell you I loved you *as well*?' said Tim.

THE OPALESCENT OPAL

A favorite stone of Queen Victoria, the opal possesses a fragile, iridescent beauty that is difficult to put into words—though we shall try. Somewhat translucent, with a pearly sheen, the opal exhibits a fascinating play of colors that flash and change with light and movement. It is this sort of iridescence that is often called "opalescence."

Like many gems, the opal has its share of accompanying superstitions. For example, in the Middle Ages a person who possessed an opal and was born in October would be the recipient of good luck. Yet one not born in October who dared wear an opal had better beware! Today, surely, anyone who owns an opal must be considered lucky. For no one owning anything as lovely—and as expensive—as an opal could ever be thought unlucky!

There are several different types: white, fire and black opals. The last type, mined in Australia, is the most rare and highly prized—and the sort that plays a part in Joyce Dingwell's *The All-the-Way Man*.

Like diamonds or rubies, fire opals are usually cut into facets; but most opals are given smoothly rounded finishes—the sort of surface that best sets off the truly unique opalescence of this lovely gemstone.

4 FREE
Harlequin Romances

TAKE THESE 4 Harlequin Romances FREE

as advertised on TV

Thrill to romantic, aristocratic Istanbul, and the tender love story of a girl who built a barrier around her emotions in ANNE HAMPSON's "Beyond the Sweet Waters" . . . a Caribbean island is the scene setting for love and conflict in ANNE MATHER's "The Arrogant Duke" . . . exciting, sun-drenched California is the locale for romance and deception in VIOLET WINSPEAR's "Cap Flamingo" . . . and an island near the coast of East Africa spells drama and romance for the heroine in NERINA HILLIARD's "Teachers Must Learn."

Harlequin Romances . . . 6 exciting novels published each month! Each month you will get to know interesting, appealing, true-to-life people . . . . You'll be swept to distant lands you've dreamed of visiting . . . . Intrigue, adventure, romance, and the destiny of many lives will thrill you through each Harlequin Romance novel.

Get all the latest books before they're sold out!

As a Harlequin subscriber you actually receive your personal copies of the latest Romances immediately after they come off the press, so you're sure of getting all 6 each month.

Cancel your subscription whenever you wish!

You don't have to buy any minimum number of books. Whenever you decide to stop your subscription just let us know and we'll cancel all further shipments.

Your FREE gift includes

- *Anne Hampson* — Beyond the Sweet Waters
- *Anne Mather* — The Arrogant Duke
- *Violet Winspear* — Cap Flamingo
- *Nerina Hilliard* — Teachers Must Learn

FREE GIFT CERTIFICATE

and Subscription Reservation

Mail this coupon today!

In the U.S.A.
1440 South Priest Drive
Tempe, AZ 85281

In Canada
649 Ontario Street
Stratford, Ontario N5A 6W2

Harlequin Reader Service:

Please send me my 4 Harlequin Romance novels FREE.
Also, reserve a subscription to the 6 NEW Harlequin
Romance novels published each month. Each month I will
receive 6 NEW Romance novels at the low price of $1.50
each (*Total–$9.00 a month*). There are no shipping and
handling or any other hidden charges. I may cancel this
arrangement at any time, but even if I do, these first 4 books
are still mine to keep.

_____

NAME   (PLEASE PRINT)

_____

ADDRESS

_____

CITY   STATE/PROV.   ZIP/POSTAL CODE

Offer not valid to present subscribers

Offer expires April 30, 1982.   B2432

Prices subject to change without notice.